M000115108

PRAISE FOR
BAD LOVE STRIKES

"An absorbing and engaging book that intertwines one of the darkest times in history with hope, ingenuity, action, adventure, and comedy. Parts of the book took me back to earlier times, when my life and dreams were encapsulated by my next meal, what was on the TV, and listening to the great music of the 60's and 70's. However, I could relate with the quest to right some wrongs, search for purpose, and strive for greater things beyond my vision. As a practicing radiation oncologist who has dealt firsthand with the recondite world of nuclear physics and its effects and interactions with everyday life, I found it fascinating and enthralling. In trying to apply these concepts to reverse the course of past human atrocities, the book appeals to all ages because of its wit and the fantasy world that you become part of. Dr. Schewe weaves together these difficult concepts with brilliance and humor."

—David A. Holladay, M.D.

"Tweens, teens, and adults will travel, discover, sing, laugh, and cry when experiencing a historic time travel mission with the Bad Love Gang (BLG). You won't have to understand time travel or Einstein's theory of relativity, because the author's imagination fills in details of this tale. If you do understand the theory, you're going to enjoy the trip! Music, laughter, and sadness are sprinkled throughout the novel, making it a fast-paced adventure. Team-building, friendship, and hope are ageless, and so is this well-crafted voyage into the time-space continuum! I am ready for the next adventure."

—Marlene Grippa

Bad Love Strikes
Kevin L. Schewe, MD, FACRO

Published August 2019
Broken Crow Ridge
Imprint of Jan-Carol Publishing, Inc.
All rights reserved
Copyright © 2019 Kevin L. Schewe, MD, FACRO

This is a work of fiction. Any resemblance to actual persons, either living or dead is entirely coincidental. All names, characters and events are the product of the author's imagination.

This book may not be reproduced in whole or part, in any manner whatsoever without written permission, with the exception of brief quotations within book reviews or articles.

ISBN: 978-1-950895-09-0
Library of Congress Control Number: 2019947891

You may contact the publisher:
Jan-Carol Publishing, Inc.
PO Box 701
Johnson City, TN 37605
publisher@jancarolpublishing.com
jancarolpublishing.com

BAD LOVE STRIKES

KEVIN L. SCHEWE, MD, FACRO

Jan-Carol
Publishing, Inc

"every story needs a book"

DEDICATION

I have been a board-certified cancer specialist practicing radiation oncology for 32 years as of July 1st, 2019. I am the youngest of three children and have two older sisters, Kathy Williams and Denise Bourg. As a cancer doctor, I know firsthand that cancer can indiscriminately affect anyone at any time. In December of 2016, cancer hit home for our family when my sister Kathy Williams was diagnosed with stage III, triple-negative breast cancer (a particularly virulent type). Kathy bravely accepted her diagnosis and steadfastly endured nearly six months of very intensive chemotherapy, followed by a double mastectomy and reconstructive surgery. She then worked hard at physically and mentally recovering from all of her treatments. I am pleased to report that she has been in a complete remission and cancer-free since late summer 2017.

For as long as I can remember, Kathy and I have shared a love for any story that involves time travel. Two years after her diagnosis of breast cancer, in early December 2018, I read the story of the Phantom Fortress and became inspired to write this book based on time travel. I actually started writing on January 14th of this year; many days later, I realized that I had started writing on Kathy's birthday. Therefore, it is only fitting and right that I dedicate this book to my sister Kathy Williams, who has been—and will continue to be—an inspiration to us all.

BAD LOVE
STRIKES

ACKNOWLEDGMENTS

For 32+ years I have worked on the front lines of cancer care as a radiation oncologist in private practice. Receiving a diagnosis of cancer and then facing the realities of staging, treatment, side effects, and recovery are challenges that are larger than life. Living with a cancer diagnosis after treatment requires a new view on life and life's priorities. I want to acknowledge the thousands of patients that I have cared for these past 32+ years—all of whom have taught me valuable lessons of life and have shown me courage beyond measure, sacrifice, love, humility, victory, the real-life occurrence of miracles, and acceptance. I am thankful to all of these patients, their families, and their loved ones; they have shown me, and continue to show me, the meaning of life here on earth.

AUTHOR'S FOREWORD

RECOMMENDED ACTION FOR ALL YOU TIME TRAVELERS OUT THERE!

In order to get the full sensory effect of traveling through time with the Bad Love Gang, I highly recommend that you download the 21-song soundtrack listed on the next page by using your iTunes, Spotify, Pandora, or Amazon Prime account. Alternatively, you could use YouTube to play each song as you are reading. As each song is introduced throughout the novel, take the time (no pun intended!) to listen to the music and enjoy the full effect of being an honorary member of the Bad Love Gang. This recommended action will be especially enjoyable during Chapter Fifteen, The Fun Part of the Flight, when each Bad Love Gang time traveler has their favorite "road song" played while the group travels into danger aboard the B-17G Flying Fortress carrying the moniker Bad Love. Do not be shy or afraid to break out and dance or to simply tap your feet as the music moves you!

Bad Love Strikes will make you feel like a teenager again and will transport you back to 1974 and 1944 as you learn about time travel, the origins of Area 51, the discovery of exotic matter, the Manhattan Project to build the world's first atomic bomb, the air war over Europe in WWII, and the Holocaust that started in Chelmno, Poland, at the very time of President Roosevelt's famous *Day of Infamy* speech, launching America into WWII. Happy reading, and remember: "Live dangerously, have fun, don't die!"

SOUNDTRACK TO *BAD LOVE STRIKES*

1. "Born to Be Wild," Steppenwolf (1968)
2. "Let's Twist Again," Chubby Checker (1961)
3. "In the Year 2525," Zagar and Evans (1968)
4. "Incense and Peppermints," Strawberry Alarm Clock (1967)
5. "I Can See Clearly Now," Johnny Nash (1972)
6. "A Horse with No Name," America (1971)
7. "Takin' Care of Business," Bachman Turner Overdrive (1974)
8. "California Dreamin'," The Mamas & the Papas (1966)
9. "C'mon and Swim," Bobby Freeman (1964)
10. "Help!" The Beatles (1965)
11. "You Keep Me Hanging On," The Supremes (1966)
12. "She's Not There," The Zombies (1964)
13. "Travelin' Band," Credence Clearwater Revival (1970)
14. "Burning Love," Elvis Presley (1972)
15. "Secret Agent Man," Johnny Rivers (1966)
16. "Goldfinger," Shirley Bassey (1964)
17. "Fly Me to the Moon," Frank Sinatra (1964)
18. "Me and Mrs. Jones," Billy Paul (1972)
19. "Theme from Shaft," Isaac Hayes (1971)
20. "Shambala," Three Dog Night (1973)
21. "Never Been Any Reason," Head East (1975)

MAIN CHARACTERS

THE BAD LOVE GANG FROM OAK RIDGE, TENNESSEE

1.   Kevin "Bubble Butt" Schafer
2.   Nathan "Bowmar" Williams
3.   Brianna "Cleopatra" Williams
4.   Jimmy "Goondoggy" Blanchert
5.   Billy "Willy" Blanchert
6.   Donny "The Runt" Legrande
7.   David "Crazy Ike" Eichenmuller
8.   Karen "Crisco" O'Sullivan
9.   Frankie "Spaghetti Head" Russo
10. Gary "the Pud" Jacobson
11. Aaron "Meatball" Eisen
12. Paul "Waldo" Thompson

ADDED BAD LOVE GANG FROM THE 1944 RESCUE MISSION

1.   Jack "Bucky" Smith
2.   Darby "Pumpkin" Nelson

THE 13 RESCUED HOLOCAUST SURVIVORS

1–3. David, Sarah and Hannah Lieb
4–5. Vadoma and Barsali Loveridge
6–7. Asher and Avigail Goldberg
8.   Benzion "Ben" Kaplan
9–13. Daniel, Mazal, Zelda and Rhoda Roth, as well as Mazal's mother, Rachel Soros

TABLE OF CONTENTS

CHAPTER ONE

THE DISCOVERY OF EXOTIC MATTER

"The only reason for time is so that everything
doesn't happen at once."
—Albert Einstein

June 17, 1942 at 10:00 PM local time, Nevada desert: Area 51

Second Lieutenant Jack "Bucky" Smith was assigned to a special U.S. Eighth Air Force operation tasked with pushing the aerodynamic limits and air battle characteristics of the new Boeing B-17F Flying Fortress, which had recently arrived on the scene in the spring of 1942. He and his crew had just test landed their B-17F after sunset at Area 51 (AKA Groom Dry Lake), which was then known as Indian Springs Airfield. The Indian Springs Airfield had been rapidly constructed and immediately brought into service by the U.S. Army Air Force about one month after Pearl Harbor was bombed in December 1941. The airfield was constructed on Groom Dry Lake, a salt flat in the southwestern Nevada desert that was remote and mainly known to the U.S. military involved in its origins. The airfield supported B-17 Flying Fortresses, B-25 Mitchells, and T-6 Texans trainer aircraft. Indian Springs was "officially" used for air-to-air gunnery training, and as a divert field for Las Vegas Army Airfield. On this Wednesday night in June 1942, something happened that forever changed the course of history for

1

Indian Springs Airfield in the remote southwestern Nevada desert, altering the destiny of Second Lieutenant Jack "Bucky" Smith as well.

Bucky was a good student and athlete, a 1936 graduate of West High School (Denver's second oldest high school) and a 1940 graduate of West Point. His uncle had taught him to fly a Boeing-Stearman Model 75 biplane in the summer of 1934, and he was forever hooked on being a pilot. After graduating cum laude from West Point in May 1940 as a second lieutenant, he immediately joined the U.S. Army Air Corps (USAAC). On June 20, 1941, the U.S. Army Air Corps became the U.S. Army Air Forces (USAAF). The U.S. Eighth Air Force was activated on January 2, 1942; Bucky was then working for the Eighth Air Force. He was celebrating his 24th birthday on this very day and had spoken to his parents by a long-distance telephone call earlier that afternoon, before his scheduled six-hour long test flight. The B-17F four-engine heavy bomber his team was tasked with testing was an improved model, upgraded from its predecessor, the B-17E. Although there were many improvements, the main difference between the E and F were the wider Hamilton Standard paddle-blade propellers, fitted to the F model to give it better performance. The B-17Fs were on a tight upcoming delivery schedule, due to begin arriving in England in August 1942. They were destined to fly in the air war against Nazi Germany throughout 1943 before being replaced by the further-improved B-17G Flying Fortresses, beginning in late 1943.

Bucky's six-hour B-17F mission that day had included a high-altitude bombing run, simulated air-to-air combat with multiple hostile "enemy" fighter aircraft trying to "shoot them down," and various high-speed dive, recovery, and turn maneuvers. Finally, close to finishing the tests, they had just completed a trial night landing at 9:30 PM local time. Just as they reached the end of their final landing approach to touch down on the salt flat runway, there was a moment of sheer panic as their electrical systems seemed to temporarily short out. Bucky was born with nerves of steel (which is how he ended up in special ops), and ignored the electrical problem while he finished the landing. The electrical problem had seemed to fix itself while they taxied to the hangar and ground maintenance, parking for the night. What they didn't know at the moment was that all electricity had been temporarily interrupted in a one-hundred-mile radius.

Planes and crews were coming and going on a nearly nonstop basis in the early days of World War II at Indian Springs Airfield. Although he was young and only a second lieutenant by rank, Bucky was the ranking officer on site that fateful Wednesday night. One of his enlisted ground crew friends, Army Sergeant Jamie Gray, was sitting in a nearby jeep and chain smoking from a pack of Chesterfields. His dog Rusty was a border collie, a breed known for their ability to withstand heat and being able to work in harsh conditions. Bucky walked up and said "Hi" to Rusty, who was resting in the back seat, and playfully scratched his ears for a minute. Bucky then sat in the jeep's passenger seat and said, "Hey, Jamie, we had a little scare on landing; all our electrical systems temporarily went down, but they came back up while we taxied."

Jamie replied, "That's crazy, because—no bullshit, Bucky—the whole base went completely dark for a few minutes! Some of the guys said that the Nazis or Japs were bombing Nevada, and I told them to cut that crap out!"

Jamie offered Bucky a cigarette and Bucky started to say, "You know I don't smo—" At that moment in time, the sky over Groom Dry Lake lit up as brightly as the light of a summer day, only to be followed by a thunderous explosion and what felt like an earthquake, followed by darkness again. In the distance, on the salt flat property adjacent to one of the long new runways under construction, they could see what

3

appeared to be a glowing site of wreckage. The few enlisted support personnel on duty at that time of the evening, along with Bucky and Jamie, jumped in their jeeps and trucks to go check out what they all assumed was a plane crash.

It was not what it seemed.

As they started their drive to the crash site, Bucky estimated that it was about 2–2.5 miles away. Groom Dry Lake (Area 51) was a bit lower in elevation at 4,409 feet than Bucky's "mile-high" home town of Denver, Colorado. The property measured approximately 3.7 miles from north to south, and 3 miles from east to west at its widest points. Two trucks and a pair of jeeps were driving parallel to each other down the salt flat, barreling along with their headlights beaming, kicking up billowing clouds of dust behind them as they all headed directly to the wreckage site. Bucky had left instructions for the staff remaining at the base to place a call to Las Vegas Army Airfield to see if the flight had originated from there, and to alert them that a plane had crashed at Indian Springs Airfield. They needed to be prepared to send an investigative team to document and deal with whatever had just happened.

It was a beautiful, clear, still, star-filled June evening in the Nevada desert, and the temperature was hovering at 75 degrees. As they drove down the salt flats in their open-air army jeep, Jamie flicked his last cigarette away, looked at Bucky, and said, "Happy birthday, buddy. I guess you won't be blowing this candle out tonight!" Bucky smiled and answered, "I'm sure you could blow it out with all your hot air, Jamie! For some reason, I don't have a good feeling about this. I have been scanning the sky, the horizon, and surroundings in front of and around us while you have been driving, and have I yet to see any sign of parachutes. This might be an ugly scene up ahead." He looked back at Rusty, who was alertly sitting up and enjoying the ride, all eyes and ears at this moment.

As they all approached within a couple hundred yards of the site, it became apparent that this was not a plane crash. When they got about one hundred yards away, Bucky motioned for everyone to stop. There was no debris field—but there was a single large, glowing object, craft, vehicle, or vessel adjacent to a future runway under construction. The object had crashed at a slight angle and created a large crater in the desert floor, partially obscuring their sight of a portion of the lower aspect of the craft's structure. Oddly, there was no fire burning, but the crash site was glowing white with a bluish tint that seemed to be emanating from some material extruding from several cracks in the hull of the damaged vessel. Bucky had better-than-perfect 20/20 vision, and could see the vague outline of what he thought could be a person examining the damage to the outer hull. Jamie offered Bucky a pair of binoculars that were under his driver's seat. Just as Bucky looked through them at the subject examining the outer hull, the subject seemed to look directly back at him. The bluish color reflected off its slightly-built body. In its oval, slightly almond-shaped face, large eyes appeared to blink at Bucky and Jamie; from a rather small mouth came a very high-pitched shrill noise that carried through and past their position. Rusty let out a continuous, primitive-sounding canine howl like never before, taking both Jamie and Bucky by surprise. Bucky watched as the subject quickly started moving toward an opening in the hull.

Just as the subject started moving, the vehicle's shape began to change. While disc-shaped flying objects had been intermittently observed and recorded since the Middle Ages, the first recorded use of the term *flying saucer* for an unidentified flying object (UFO) had occurred in the United States exactly twelve years prior to this night, on June 17, 1930. On that night, people in Texas and Oklahoma witnessed a bright red glow that was described as a "flaming flying saucer," and may have been a comet or meteor. What Bucky and his small team of enlisted soldiers were looking at from one hundred yards away was a metallic-appearing space craft that glowed white, and the blue tint was emanating from the material that was leaking or extruding from breaches in the hull due to crash damage. The vehicle was comprised of two circular or disc shaped hulls; the larger, lower disc was vertically connected to a smaller upper disc by a funnel shaped structure. Bucky's B-17F Flying Fortress had a wingspan of nearly 104 feet, and he guesstimated that the diameter of the lower disc exceeded that width by 20–30 feet, while the upper disc was slightly less than 100 feet in diameter. This made the vehicle very large, but not exactly massive in an unearthly way. The vehicle's shape was changing; the middle of the funnel shaped structure connecting the upper and lower discs telescoped as the upper disc moved upward, creating more separation between the two discs. The middle of the funnel structure simultaneously began to glow a brighter blue and make what was at first a soft whirr. It was certainly a sight to behold, and like nothing that Bucky or his group of enlisted men had ever seen on earth in this life.

At this moment in time, Bucky began to act on instinct and impulse. He knew that he was the only officer at the crash site, and therefore fully in charge about what to do next—or not do. He instructed Jamie and the other jeep's driver to drive forward within 25 yards of the object, and angle their headlights on the lower hull at the open entrance. He told the other two trucks to drive around and keep an eye on the opposite side of the craft. As the two jeeps got within 25 yards and stopped, Bucky told Jamie that he was going in, and that if he did not come out soon, to hold their ground until more help came.

Jamie looked at him and asked incredulously, "Are you plum crazy, Bucky? You have no idea what kinda shit you are getting into!" Bucky checked to make sure his Colt 45 caliber ACP service pistol was holstered and ready, then replied, "For some reason, I'm not afraid. I want to go see what this is all about, but I don't want to put anyone else in jeopardy. Besides, I'm in charge—and no guts, no glory!" He then jumped out of the jeep and headed for the open entrance in the lower hull. When Bucky departed, Rusty took his place, sitting next to Jamie in the front of the jeep with his ears pointed straight up. The dog quivered, intently watching Bucky.

Bucky ran toward the lower hull's open entrance as the upper disc was still in motion. The whirring noise coming from the expanding telescopic funnel structure connecting the two discs was growing noticeably louder. As he came to the entrance he slowed down and noticed that the hull did have a white glow, like it was plugged in and active. From the corner of his eye he identified the breach in the hull that the subject he'd seen through the binoculars had been examining. The material leaking through that breach was almost a neon blue and definitely the source of the blue tint they had seen in the distance. The thought occurred to him that the same material was probably making the funnel structure above appear blue as well.

When he came through the hull entrance, he slowed to a walk and stopped about ten feet inside to take an assessment of his surroundings. He was in a circular hallway that apparently wrapped around the circumference of the lower hull. He moved to his left and noticed doorways on both sides that he could only describe as similar to elevator doors, but these were very sleek and shiny. He chose to keep moving in the direction of the whirring noise, which was continuing to grow louder. It seemed to be coming from the center of the lower hull. He moved clockwise along the circular hallway, and knew that he would have to pick a doorway on his right to continue to the center of the vessel. Strangely, he thought that even at this moment he was more excited to discover the truth than afraid for his own safety.

The noise was getting ever louder as he came to a much larger set of doors on his right, unlike any of the prior doorways. He wasn't sure how to open them, but inwardly felt that time was of the essence. With the vehicle changing shape and the noise continually growing louder, he just sensed something major was going to happen soon. He pushed on the doorway and tried to pry it open, but to no avail. Then he chose to "dance" across the doorway, waving his arms widely like a crazy man; the doorway opened, both sides literally disappearing into the walls with a flash. Bucky audibly said to himself, "I can dance! If you get stuck again, remember to dance, Bucky!"

He wasn't quite prepared for what he witnessed next. He walked through the large double doorway and onto a large circular balcony that was open to the middle of the vessel. The walls were comprised of integrated and complex machinery, all of which was active and running. His senses were overloading, but he tried to stay focused. Ahead in the center opening of the middle of the vessel was the bluish glowing funnel structure connecting the discs, and Bucky could tell it was making the whirring sound. He went to the edge of the balcony and looked down. There was a large, circular machine on the floor that looked like a race track, and the subject he had seen from afar was calmly walking into the middle. The funnel structure was closing in from above, lining up to dock with the racetrack. The wide mouth of the funnel made for docking with the racetrack was transparent. There were a total of six beings seated in the eye of the racetrack. The one Bucky had seen outside sat with what appeared to be its mate and two smaller children, both of whom had rounder faces than their parents. The other two beings were seated together and facing each other. Bucky was sure that they had some type of clothing on that had a reflective sheen and appeared to be skin tight, but it certainly did not seem to limit their flexibility or movements.

The wide part of the funnel was fully docked with the racetrack by this time; the noise was higher pitched and louder than ever, and reaching a crescendo. Bucky instinctively yelled to the six beings below, "Hey, I need to talk to you!" One of the two children looked up at Bucky at that moment with eyes wide open and waved. At that same moment, all six beings literally disappeared into thin air; the eye of the racetrack was suddenly empty. The whirr faded and the neon bluish color of the funnel connection dimmed, but continued to glow. All the integrated machines along the circular walls turned off. On the outside of the craft, the white glow also faded out, as if the power had been disconnected. However, the bluish material coming from the breaches in the hull still glowed, as if it had a life of its own.

Bucky, still staring at the center of the machine, was exhausted. As he took a deep breath, he noticed a strange odor that quickly dissipated before he could define it in words. He told himself he would remember to mention that little fact in his report of this evening's events. The inside of the vessel was still dimly lit, as if on emergency power, and Bucky was able to make his way back out. By now, the entire group of enlisted men was waiting for him, and to a person they were all relieved to see Bucky exiting the space craft uninjured and in one piece.

Bucky spoke first. "It looks like our 'friends' are gone. There were six of them, and they literally got transported away into thin air by a machine inside that ship. One of the little ones waved at me the moment they disappeared!"

Jamie asked, "What did they look like?"

Bucky replied, "One thing I can tell you, there must not be any fat cells in their bodies: all of them are skinny. I guess they don't have barbequed ribs, ice cream malts, chocolate bars, or beer on Mars and Pluto!"

"I'm not going if there's no beer!" Jamie declared.

As they all stood and marveled at the alien space craft, a few more support personnel began to arrive at the scene. Bucky quickly pulled everyone together and said, "As the ranking officer here at this moment, no one is to go aboard that ship tonight or at any time without prior permission. I want an armed guard duty patrol surrounding this place until I can get some higher-level brass here from Las Vegas, tomorrow morning. No one is leaving this base or coming onto this base until further notice. Gentlemen, we are on lockdown! No one can know about this; *no one*, understand? That is an *order!*"

The entire group collectively answered, "Yes *sir!*" Bucky had earned their respect with his fearless and aggressive approach to tonight's events. As sergeant, Jamie was second in command of the group of enlisted men on hand; he carried out Bucky's orders to set up the guard duty for the night.

Bucky returned to the base and contacted the commanding officer at Las Vegas Army Airfield. The next morning, everything began to change at Indian Springs Airfield as the reality of the alien spaceship crash began to sink in. By direct order from President Franklin D. Roosevelt the following day, June 18, 1942, this alien spacecraft crash site and its adjacent runway under construction became the nation's highest-level designated top secret. There was no practical way for the alien spacecraft to be moved; it was too big, too heavy, and too top secret. Trying to rapidly disassemble it was not even a viable option. The decision was quickly made to build a very large hanger around it with a fully supporting, top secret military base next to it and the adjacent runway under construction. The strategy was designed to hide it in plain sight, providing strict, impenetrable military protection from anyone or anything that might ever try to gain future access, and to provide an environment for the nation's brightest minds to learn its secrets.

For his part of spontaneous bravery, quick thinking, and discovery, Bucky was elevated two full ranks to *Captain* Jack 'Bucky' Smith at the young age of 24. In late October 1942, Bucky was summoned to the White House and spent the night in the Lincoln Bedroom. That night, he ate dinner with President Franklin D. Roosevelt and FDR's most trusted, top scientific adviser, Mr. Vannevar Bush. He detailed the entire story of the evening's events, giving his eyewitness account from that fateful night of June 17, 1942, directly to the two of them. It was an amazing night for the young Air Force captain from Denver, Colorado.

Before leaving the next day, Bucky was escorted to the Oval Office, where he again met with just FDR and Bush. FDR said to Bucky, "Son, because of your skills as a special ops pilot and the secrets that you carry, I need you to join a top-secret military program that we just got underway earlier this month."

"Mr. President, I would be honored to help in whatever capacity that would serve you and our country the best," Bucky answered.

"That's perfect. You will only get to know as much as is necessary to do your job effectively. The program is code named The White Hole Project; beyond the three of us seated in this room, there are precious few people who know of its existence. Let's keep it that way! Bucky, you carry on with your work for now, and Mr. Bush will contact you when he needs you. Thank you for your service," FDR concluded.

Bucky enthusiastically replied, "Yes *sir!*" shook hands with both men, and then departed.

President Roosevelt looked at Vannevar and said, "I like that young man from Denver, Colorado. After all he has been through, he is a straight arrow, and not full of himself. His record is spotless. I trust him. When you and your team have the White Hole Project ready to test, I want Bucky to be your first test pilot."

Vannevar agreed with that assessment. "Mr. President, we have more than enough of the blue exotic matter safe in our possession, and we are gaining on the time travel technology on paper and in theory. I am working on the White Hole Project construction timetable right now."

FDR thanked Bush and concluded their discussion with, "As you well know, this meeting never happened. Now go back to work."

CHAPTER TWO

THE MANHATTAN PROJECT
AND THE WHITE HOLE PROJECT

"Imagination is more important than knowledge.
Knowledge is limited. Imagination encircles the world."
—Albert Einstein

German physicists discovered uranium fission in December 1938, and reported their discovery to the world on January 6, 1939. Their results were quickly corroborated and confirmed to be true. Hungarian physicist Leo Szilard realized that the fission (splitting apart) of heavy atoms would create nuclear chain reactions that could yield vast amounts of energy for good—electrical power generation—or for bad—atomic bombs with more destructive power than ever before known to man. Szilard's esteemed colleague Albert Einstein gained widespread fame and recognition when he won the Nobel Prize in physics in 1921. He was internationally respected for his knowledge and expertise in the field of physics, plus he had a personal relationship with President Franklin D. Roosevelt. Together, Szilard and Einstein crafted a letter that was signed by Einstein and delivered directly to Roosevelt on October 11, 1939. The letter warned that Germany was pursuing an atomic bomb, and urged Roosevelt to take whatever steps were necessary for the United States to become the first nation with the atomic bomb. After reading the Szilard/Einstein letter, Roosevelt was said to have declared, "This requires action!"

On October 9, 1941, Roosevelt made the decision to pursue an atomic bomb pilot program. On December 7, 1941, The Empire of Japan surprise attacked the United States at Pearl Harbor, pulling the United States into World War II. One day before the alien ship crashed at Area 51 (AKA Groom Dry Lake, or Indian Springs Airfield) on June 16, 1942, Roosevelt had approved the all-out effort for the U.S. to be the first country to build the atomic bomb. The U.S. effort to build the world's first atomic bomb was code-named The Manhattan Project. This step by President Franklin D. Roosevelt launched a scientific journey of gigantic proportions, opening the door to the Nuclear Age that we all know and live in today. The circle of people who actually knew the objective and timeline of the Manhattan Project was extremely small. In fact, FDR's own vice president, Harry Truman—who ultimately chose to use the atomic bomb against Japan to end World War II—did not learn of the Manhattan Project or the bomb's existence until he was sworn in as president after FDR's death. What has not been known until recently was that there was a separate, even more secretive project running parallel to the Manhattan Project, one that far fewer people knew even existed.

Thursday, October 1, 1942 at 7:00 PM local time:
The White House

On the evening of October 1, 1942, President Roosevelt and Vannevar Bush had scheduled a private dinner meeting with Albert Einstein at the White House. After exchanging pleasantries and catching up socially, FDR got down to the business at hand.

Roosevelt stated, "Gentlemen, I am concerned about the race we have entered to become the first nation with an atomic bomb. If Adolf

Hitler and the Germans get the atomic bomb first—and we have reason to believe that they could be ahead of us at this moment—the world would be faced with an impossible choice. We know that Hitler and his Nazi Party fully desire and are actively and aggressively pressing their will for world domination. It is an untenable thought for them to be the first to get the atomic bomb and carry out their hideous plans. I therefore would propose to you both that prudence calls for us to have a backup plan to The Manhattan Project, in case we lose this race."

"You certainly have my curiosity aroused, Mr. President, and as you know, I am a big fan of prudence. So, what do you have in mind?" Einstein enquired.

Roosevelt answered, "Albert, I would like to commission you, along with the help of only your smallest circle of absolutely necessary, most trusted colleagues, to work with Vannevar to construct a usable time travel machine, code named The White Hole Project. If the Germans win the race to acquire the atomic bomb first, then the White Hole Project will become America's fallback plan to foil the German's achievement and prevent their quest for world domination."

Roosevelt, his family and Einstein were long-time friends. Einstein, not always known to be particularly fond of authority, did however respect FDR and looked at him with a bit of surprise and wonderment on this October evening. He thought for a minute, then responded, "Mr. President, I know you, and I know that you are not one to make a request like this out of thin air. It was Ludwig Flamm who first used the phrase *white hole* back in 1916. Flamm postulated that a white hole could be a theoretical time reversal of a black hole, and that entrances to both black and white holes could be connected by a spacetime passageway. What you are requesting tonight exists only in brilliant minds and theory. In fact, not too long ago, Nathan Rosen and I proposed the idea of spacetime bridges that could connect two different points in spacetime. My theory of general relativity mathematically predicts the presence of spacetime conduits, which would have two funnel openings connected by a passageway. The practical problem for all this to work is stability: making the passageway stay open long enough for spacetime travel to occur. That passageway would be inherently unstable, and prone to rapidly collapse. It would take some other-worldly exotic matter to hold the connection open for spacetime travelers to effectively—and safely, I might add—go back and forth through spacetime conduits."

The room was very quiet for a moment. FDR seemed to be deep in thought; Bush had decided to mainly listen and take orders from these two men of historic destiny. Then the president spoke. "Albert, I believe that we will find that your physics theories continue to prove true. What I tell you next is a secret that you must promise to take to your grave. On June seventeenth of this year, an alien space ship crashed in the remote southwest Nevada desert in an area called Groom Dry Lake, or Indian Springs Airfield. The occupants of the vessel used what we believe to be a spacetime machine to return to where they came from. The vessel itself and the machine that they used for their escape are lined with a glowing blue exotic material that none of our scientists have yet been able to identify or accurately characterize. It is possible that this is what you are referring to, matter that is needed for stability of spacetime travel. That is certainly beyond my intelligence, but exactly why I wanted you here tonight. I want you to go to Nevada with whomever you need to examine the alien ship and its contents, learn what you can from all of it, and show us how to build a usable time-travel machine. I'm talking more than usual tonight, but I have a lot to say."

Einstein smiled. "Since I am taking this secret to my grave, Mr. President, you have plenty of time to say whatever you desire!"

They all laughed and Roosevelt continued, "I appointed General Leslie Groves the military commander of The Manhattan Project last month. He has already instructed the U.S. Army Corps of Engineers to purchase fifty-nine thousand acres of land along the Clinch River in East Tennessee, near Knoxville. The area has vast tracts of land, water, electricity, and needed workers. It is the perfect location to build a secret city we are calling Site X, which will become the epicenter of our efforts to build the world's first atomic bomb. Soon, the largest building in the world under one roof will be located there, processing the fuel needed for the atomic bomb. It is on this massive construction site that we will build our White Hole Project time-travel machine. Only a handful of people can know about this project; for all appearances, everyone will automatically assume that it is part of the atomic bomb project and associated construction. Once it is far enough along, we will seal it off and give it a separate entrance. Vannevar, all the money we spend on this White Hole Project will come from the Manhattan Project's funding. There will be no financial footprint leading to the White Hole Project." Vannevar nodded his acknowledgement.

Einstein inquired further: "I believe I know the answer, but I always like to ask lots of questions. Why are you placing a stricter cloak of secrecy around the White Hole Project, around time travel, than the atomic bomb Manhattan Project, Mr. President?"

Roosevelt responded, "I am pleased that you asked that question, Albert, because I have given this some good measure of thought. I am somewhat conflicted by this contingency plan. It seems to me that a bomb, whether big or small, dependably blows stuff up, knocks things down, and destroys a portion of a certain geography and people in its proximity. All that destruction can presumably be rebuilt over time. However, I happen to believe that time travel in the wrong hands could be far more devastating to world history and mankind than atomic weaponry. The ultimate consequences or damages of changing human history by using time travel seems potentially far more widely reaching and difficult to quantify, or even fathom the outcome. But that said, the thought of Hitler and the Nazi Party having the atomic bomb first is also impossible to fathom."

Einstein then said, "I tend to imagine the world as how it could be, Mr. President, while you have to deal with the world as it is. I am grateful for the opportunities life has brought my way. I will help you, and I plan to take this secret to my grave, a very long time from now!" Roosevelt assured Einstein that Vannevar would provide his unlimited assistance as needed, and then thanked the two of them for an interesting and productive evening.

As Einstein and Bush parted ways at the door, Einstein commented, "Vannevar, you hardly said a word all night long."

Vannevar replied, "I learned a lot tonight and feel smarter for having listened well."

"Fair enough, Vannevar, fair enough," Einstein conceded.

CHAPTER THREE
THE PHANTOM FORTRESS

"The process of scientific discovery is, in effect,
A continual flight from wonder."
—Albert Einstein

Kortenberg, Belgium, Tuesday, November 21, 1944

This story is true and occurred late in the afternoon at a British Royal Airforce (RAF) airbase, antiaircraft unit near Kortenberg, Belgium. The on-site British gunners and spotters were caught by surprise, shocked to see a gleaming new B-17G Flying Fortress descending steadily toward them with its landing gear down, rapidly approaching their gunnery position. The British soldiers put a quick call into the operations center, only to learn that no such landing had been requested, either as routine or emergency. Yet this formidable American Eighth Air Force 4-engine, heavy bomber, a symbol of Allied strength and might, was barreling in hard and fast for a landing. Could this be a captured plane commandeered by the Germans, being used as a modern Trojan Horse?

The B-17G flew by the antiaircraft gunnery position and made a perfect three-point landing in the adjacent plowed field. At the end of its landing run, one of the plane's wingtips dipped and dug into the earth, causing one of the propellers to buckle and the plane to ground

19

loop before coming to a complete stop. Everyone on the ground watching with astonishment saw that the three undamaged engines continued to run, the propellers whirling smoothly. To make matters even more mysterious, not a single person ever emerged from the plane. A full twenty minutes subsequently elapsed, and still there was no sign of life; no one came out of the giant bomber, and the three engines continued to run. Was it some kind of a trap? Were the occupants so badly injured (dying, or already dead) that they physically could not exit the plane?

After the twenty minutes passed, a lone British army officer named John V. Crisp apprehensively approached the plane to investigate. Crisp looked around the plane and discovered an entrance hatch under the front aspect of the fuselage. He opened the hatch and bravely climbed inside the plane, at which point the plot began to thicken exponentially. To Crisp's mind-numbing amazement, there was no one on board. He could find no one in the cockpit of the plane; it was empty (but there were signs of recent occupation). The plane was a ghost ship. Using the process of trial and error, Crisp managed to shut down and turn off the three engines that had continued to run. He then proceeded to carefully inspect what became known as The Phantom Fortress.

Crisp was worried that he would discover dead or dying men as he began to search the rest of the interior of the B-17. Why else would no one get off the plane after it landed? The Major couldn't find a soul; what he did find were about twelve neatly wrapped parachute packs, ready to strap on—but obviously hadn't been used. How was this possible?

The parachutes were still there, but the entire crew was gone. How do you leave a plane in flight without a parachute, and how does that plane land safely with no one on board? Despite these unanswered questions, the major later commented, "Evidence of fairly recent occupation was everywhere."

Major Crisp continued his observations, saying, "I went to the navigator's station. The bomber's log was lying open on the navigator's desk, and the last words written were *Bad flak*." Also on the navigator's desk was the daily code book, which provided the crew with the identifying colors and letters of the day, used for communicating with the other crews flying the same mission. Located in the body of the plane were several leather flying jackets with their easily recognizable fur collars. Why would anyone bail out of the plane in November without their coat? *This is crazy!* Major Crisp thought. In addition, there were several chocolate bars lying around—some of them half-eaten. Finally, Crisp made a note that the Sperry bombsight remained intact, with its cover sitting neatly beside it, which was typical if the bombardier had been on his bombing run. One thing that Crisp left out of his official report was the strange smell or odor that temporarily permeated the plane's interior when he first entered. He could not quite describe it before it dissipated and was gone. He did not want to further embellish an already unbelievable reality.

The U.S. Eighth Air Force Service Command, headquartered in Belgium, subsequently sent a crew of personnel to investigate the B-17 Phantom Fortress. They checked the bomber's serial number and discovered that the plane was part of the 91st Bomber Group and astonishingly, the plane's crew was already at their base in East Anglia, England. They were part of a mission to bomb Merseburg, Germany oil targets, including the high-value target known as the Leuna synthetic oil refinery. Their plane had reportedly developed engine trouble just before reaching the target area.

According to the report made, the new and yet-to-be-named B-17G—on only its third mission since being delivered—was not able to keep altitude with the other bombers in its group on the bombing run. In addition, the bomb racks were not functioning properly. They indicated that the plane took two flak hits, one that directly knocked out the number three engine and another that hit the bomb bay. The first miracle of the flight was that the bombs did not go off; the crew had reported a "tremendous flash of light" when the flak hit.

The pilot did not think that they could make it back to England, so he set their course for Brussels, Belgium. Then a second engine failed, and they were losing altitude. As they reached Belgium's airspace, the pilot ordered the crew to bail out while he put the plane on autopilot—he was the last one to leave. They expected that the plane would soon crash, but they lost sight of it as it flew into the clouds. The entire crew were picked up by British infantrymen when they landed, and they had returned to England. They assumed that their B-17G crashed and perished.

Unknown to the crew, their plane continued to fly on its own and then landed, intact, by itself at Kortenberg, Belgium near Brussels. This is where the investigation doesn't squarely match with reality. The crew on the ground where the plane had landed witnessed all four engines running on approach, one engine failing after it hit the ground on landing, which ruined the propeller. The odds that an unmanned, four-engine, WWII, B-17 bomber steadily losing altitude with two engines that had already failed would then spontaneously have those failed engines restart all by themselves and work again, make it that far, and then land at a friendly base in a flat, plowed field, with no human intervention, are infinitesimal. Any qualified pilot will tell you that that the odds of winning the lottery are far better than this amazing but true story. In addition to the long-shot odds of the plane safely landing itself with all the engines running, all the parachutes were documented to be still on board, and the damage report by the personnel on the ground did not match the flight crew's damage report during the mission.

Now, while the above story is a true and documented mystery from the annals of World War II, the story that follows is what really happened both inside and outside the B-17 Phantom Fortress that fateful day in November 1944. The plane carried the name Bad Love that day, and the moment that it touched down in Kortenberg, Belgium, fully intact, there was a complete crew on board. The smell that Major Crisp detected on entering the plane... Well, that was the smell of time travel!

CHAPTER FOUR

THE BAD LOVE GANG ASSEMBLES FOR ADVENTURE

"Live dangerously, have fun, don't die."
—The Bad Love Gang Motto

Sunday morning June 09, 1974, Oak Ridge, Tennessee

It had been a wild Saturday night at the Schafer home on Hemlock Lane; my parents, Larry and Gloria, had entertained about twenty of their best friends for a "Welcome to summer 1974" party. Party central was our three-bedroom, one-bathroom, ranch-style home. The finished basement was lined with tongue and groove knotty pine paneled walls. The center attraction in the basement was a finished bar with a mirrored back wall, highlighting shelves for glasses, liquor, and wine. Four perfect height bar stools sat in front. One of my uncles owned a jukebox distributorship and as a result, we had a Wurlitzer style jukebox in one corner of the basement, replete with a fantastic mix of 1960's and then-current 1970's 45 RPM records—but it also had its share of Frank Sinatra and Dean Martin as well.

My parents were popular, fun, and had too many friends to count; when they threw a party, no one missed it! When my parents were not entertaining, my two older sisters, Kathy and Denise, often had their friends over to dance to the jukebox and party the night away. Growing up this way—watching my parents and sisters party and dance—mentally imprinted yours truly, Kevin "Bubble Butt" (or BB) Schafer, with every top-40 song from the late '50s, '60s and early '70s. Now, in mid-1974 at the ripe age of 15-and-a-half, I was building my own 45 RPM record collection. Ever since I can remember, I've had a "music brain:" I related popular songs to certain people, friends, events, and life experiences. I could be having a conversation with anyone, at any time, and something will be said that turns my music brain on like that jukebox in our basement!

Growing up in Oak Ridge, Tennessee was great! We had a population just over 28,000 in 1974, but basically had easy access to the metropolitan "big city life" of Knoxville, 25 miles to the east. Oak Ridge, established in 1942 and home of the famous World War II Manhattan Project, built to develop the world's first atomic bomb, was known variously as the Secret City, the Atomic City, the Ridge, and the City Behind the Fence. All my friends and I loved all those names. It was so cool to say, "I live in the Secret City," or "I live in the City Behind the Fence" when someone asked, "Where do you live?" It automatically stimulated many interesting conversations. In addition, you can use the word *atomic* as an adjective with any word to make it sound "big and bad," and we used that adjective liberally!

Some crazy things happened in my home town of Oak Ridge during the evolution of the enormous Manhattan project in World War II. For example, the Y-12 Plant was built in Oak Ridge to separate the isotope uranium-235 (the one that can be split by fission to release vast amounts of energy for atomic bombs or electricity) from natural uranium, which consists almost entirely of the isotope uranium-238. During construction of the powerful magnets required for the separation process, there was a nationwide, wartime shortage of copper. To get those magnets built, the Army Corps of Engineers had to "borrow"

14,700 tons of silver bullion from the United States Treasury, to be used as a substitute for the copper. Who *borrows* 14,700 tons (that's 29,400,000 pounds) of silver?! By 1974, the Y-12 site was being used for nuclear weapons processing and materials storage. The site of the Manhattan project had become the home of the Oak Ridge National Laboratory, a nuclear, high-tech, and national security research establishment.

After the war, Oak Ridge settled in as a place that was chock-full of highly educated people, academics and highly-skilled laborers who had worked on the Manhattan project. My group of neighborhood friends that I had grown up with since early childhood were all typical teenagers, but came from families that were well-educated, trained in special skills, or both. From a young age, we called ourselves the Bad Love Gang, and we were a rambunctious group of teenagers bent on finding our next wild adventure! We all went to Oak Ridge High School, and were known there as the Wildcats. It was the only public high school in Oak Ridge, Tennessee and was established in 1943 to educate the children of the Manhattan Project workers.

During the post-war period, Oak Ridge became one of the leaders in the desegregation movement in the South. On September 6, 1955, a total of 42 African American students attended the first day of school at Oak Ridge High School and were photographed by Life Magazine. Oak Ridge became the first high school in the southern United States to integrate after the U.S. Supreme Court's 1954 Brown v. Board of Education decision. We were all very proud of our desegregation leadership heritage.

Everyone in our esteemed neighborhood Bad Love Gang had been given a nickname in early childhood. We showed no mercy in our youthful evolutionary assignment of nicknames to each other based on body habits, personality traits, or noticeable physical or character "defects." I (Kevin Schafer) was graced with strong, fast sprinter's legs as a young man. Those legs originated from rather prominent and well-rounded male buttocks that quickly earned me the nickname Bubble Butt, or BB for short. I had been precocious since childhood, learning to read profusely at age four and taking sixth grade math in second grade. I am not a genius, but close to it on the bell-shaped IQ scale, and able to relate very well and be very comfortable with real geniuses like my best friend, Nathan "Bowmar" Williams. I also have a big heart and related well to our entire group of Bad Love friends. I am a problem solver, a risk taker, and love designing strategies that win. In general, my role with the Bad Love Gang was to plot and plan our various childhood and teenage adventures from start to finish, making sure that everyone felt included and important in those plans.

My alarm went off at 9:30 AM that Sunday morning. After getting up to go to the bathroom, I realized that we were not going to church that day because my parents were still asleep, recovering from the Schafer "Welcome to summer 1974" party the night before. I could hear the Magnavox (my parents loved the brand) color console TV playing in our breezeway, and headed that way. It was called a breezeway because there were floor to ceiling, louvered glass windows on either side of the room that cranked open to let the breeze freely flow through the space. The floor in that room had this crazy blue-green, deep-pile, shag carpeting with great padding underneath, making it an excellent floor to sprawl on. My two sisters, Kathy and Denise—both home from college for the summer—were both out of bed, eating cereal and watching TV in the breezeway.

As I walked in there, the Sunday morning news was playing on the Magnavox TV and the newscaster was reporting: "President Nixon is departing tomorrow for a nine-day trip to the Middle East. It will mark the first time an American president has toured the Arab countries and Israel while in office. Government officials believe that Mr. Nixon will further improve Arab-American relations, and also pledge continued American support for Israel." As soon as I heard all that, I said, "I'm turning this Tricky Dick news story off. Why are you two listening to this political crap on such a nice, beautiful Sunday morning anyway?" Denise answered that they'd just turned the TV on and that's what was playing.

I then took a minute to stare at my two sisters. Their hair (Kathy was blonde and Denise was brunette) looked like they had both plugged their fingers into the 220-volt socket meant for powering our kitchen oven. As their bratty little brother, I commented, "You both look like the twin brides of Frankenstein this morning! What happened? Did you get struck by lightning last night or what?"

Kathy responded, "Thanks, Kev; you don't exactly look like Prince Charming yourself! Mom and Dad were partying all night with their friends in the basement, and at about four or five AM, Dad decided he had to cook breakfast for the whole group. Denise and I hardly got any sleep, with all that noise going all night long!" (Kathy and Denise shared a bedroom and the door to their shared bedroom opened directly to the kitchen table sitting area.)

Using my reasonably believable John Wayne impersonation, I drawled, "Well, welcome to summer 1974, little ladies! It's time to get a move on, because we're burning daylight!"

The Schafer home on Hemlock Lane had an open-door policy for all my friends and my two sister's friends. As I finished teasing my two sisters, my best friend, Nathan "Bowmar" Williams, walked in and said "Hi" to all of us. He looked at Kathy and Denise and said, "Wow, what happened to the two of you last night?"

Denise smiled at him and replied, "Don't get started with us, Bowmar, or you're gonna be in for a painful day!" Bowmar, nearly

16 years old, was a certified genius with an IQ somewhere north of 140. He was African-American and the product of a father who was a nuclear physicist at Oak Ridge National Laboratory, and a mother who was an attorney working in Knoxville. Nathan got his nickname because of his high IQ and the first mass-produced pocket calculator, commonly called the Bowmar Brain, had hit the market in late 1971. The Bowmar brand soon became one of the world's largest selling pocket calculator brands in the early '70s. Nathan, who had purchased and regularly used one of those calculators at school very early on, landed the nickname Bowmar almost immediately. You might tend to think of a genius like him as being "nerdy," but Bowmar was a nicely dressed, handsome teenager who slayed the women first with his good looks, then with his uncanny intelligence. Bowmar and his 17-year-old sister, Brianna "Cleopatra" Williams, were both long-time members of the Bad Love Gang. Brianna was a total social butterfly with a high social IQ; she managed to become the queen of any social circle she entered, so we had called her Cleopatra ever since I can remember.

As I started to ask Bowmar what he was up to, we heard a motorcycle pull up in the driveway, which was right outside the breezeway. It was Goondoggy, on his new 1974 Honda CR125M Elsinore. In 1974, dirt bikes were a hot commodity. Motorcycling for fun was big business, and we all lived and grew up in a neighborhood next to a sizeable patch of woods within easy reach to go off road riding and dirt biking, with tons of opportunity to explore for hours and days on end! We had all had dirt bikes since we were eleven or twelve years old and almost to a person, we were all fans of the Honda motorcycle brand. Goondoggy walked in and announced, "Hey guys! I called the rest of the gang, and we are taking a ride this fine Sunday morning!" He stopped at the breezeway door, looked at Kathy and Denise and commented, "Now that's an atomic bad hair day if I ever saw one!"

29

Kathy responded this time. "Goondoggy, I'm gonna pull your underwear over your face in about two minutes!"

Jimmy "Goondoggy" Blanchert grew up next door to me from the time we were knee high to puddle ducks. I am not entirely sure how Jimmy got his nickname of Goondoggy, but we all loved to scream it out whenever he appeared on the scene. He had an older brother, Billy "Willy" Blanchert, who was also on his way to our house, as were Crazy Ike and the Runt at that moment. Goondoggy was a long, lanky kid with boundless energy who was always up for adventure, no matter what the risk. Some kids just grow up fearless; Goondoggy knew no fear from the time we knew how to say our names and play outside together. For example, I saw my very first snake when we were four or five years old; he shoved it in my face and said, "Hey Kev, look at what I found!" He was holding this eighteen-inch garter snake by the neck and trying to see what that snake's skinny little tongue felt like, protruding in and out against his cheek. Then he thought that I'd like to feel that slivery little snake tongue on my cheek. I didn't know anything about snakes, other than this situation did not feel warm and fuzzy—it felt a bit dangerous. I barked, "Get that thing out of my face, or I'm gonna stomp it *and* you for good!"

Billy "Willy" Blanchert was Goondoggy's big brother in the sense that he was a little over two years older at seventeen, and he did have a bit more wisdom. Willy pulled up next, riding his 1973 Honda SL 125, which was the same model bike as I was riding at that time. I was great friends with both of them, because Willy appealed to my intellect and Goondoggy appealed to my sense of wild adventure. Willy was a slightly built, skinny kid who was the polar opposite of Goondoggy in many ways. He wouldn't take a risk if it hit him alongside the head and his life depended on it. In fact, Willy went to great lengths to calculate whether or not any of our childhood plans stood a whimper of a chance at succeeding. He invariably tried to stand in the way of many of our adventures, only to be outvoted and then grudgingly go along for the ride.

Willy and I shared a love of all aviation related to World War II. Growing up together, we had built model airplanes of every famous World War II aircraft, including Boeing B-17s (Flying Fortress), B-24s (Liberator), B-29s (Super Fortress), Spitfires, Mustangs, Thunderbolts, Corsairs, Japanese Zeroes, German Me-109s, etc. In the mid-1960s, we had watched the *Twelve O'Clock High* TV series together as little boys. We would develop elaborate imaginary flight plans to bomb Nazi Germany targets while flying our B-17 Flying Fortress model airplanes in our hands, making every conceivable sound effect as we went. The dialogue would go something like this: "Pilot to gunners, keep your eyes peeled for Bandits! We are ready to make our bombing run. Bombardier, the plane is yours; put those bombs in their Nazi butts and let's get the hell out of here!" Then enemy fighter planes would attack, and we would make 50-caliber machine gun noises as we shot German fighter planes out of the sky from the waist gunners, ball turret, top turret, and tail gunner positions. Usually our B-17s would be hit and damaged, but we could still fly and limped back home across the English Channel to our fictitious airbase in England (actual B-17s could take a lot of battle damage and still fly). We even had post-flight discussions about how successful the bomb targeting was that day!

As we got older my Uncle Woody, who had been a B-24 Liberator Pilot in WWII, taught both Willy and me how to fly his Model 35 Beechcraft Bonanza. We shared the love of learning to fly and flying planes. After turning age 16, Willy became quite the audiophile and could wire any car for maximum sound and theater-like sound reproduction. Whatever technology was new, he was on it! This would come in handy later on, when we really needed his expertise. Willy strolled into the house carrying a 45 RPM record in his hand, and proceeded to get it ready to play on my parents Magnavox console stereo, which was against the wall to the right of the front door. When he came to the breezeway door, Denise looked at him and said, "Willy, if you say *anything* about our hair this morning, Kathy and I are going out to the driveway and slit your tires!"

Willy responded, "You know me better than that, Denise. I'm the good guy, and I'm sure that Goondoggy has already said something about your electrified hairdos! Besides, I have some music to play to get us ready to ride this morning!" Willy then turned on the music, the 1968 classic biker song from Steppenwolf's self-titled album, **"Born to Be Wild."**

We all rocked out, lip syncing and dancing to that music as it played. With that solid piece of motivation, I threw on a pair of blue jeans and we all headed out the front door. I told Bowmar that he could ride with me and rolled my 1973 Honda SL 125 out of the garage. As I did so, Karen "Crisco" O'Sullivan walked up to see where we were all headed off to this morning.

Karen "Crisco" O'Sullivan grew up across the street from me, Goondoggy and Willy. She was the product of strong Irish-Catholic parents, and was the oldest of eleven children by the time her parents maxed out. Karen was super cute with blonde hair, blue eyes, a voice mature for her age, and a perfect body—except we all thought that her butt was a little too big for her torso, so we nicknamed her Crisco, for "fat in the can." Given the fact that she was the oldest child in a large family and both her parents worked full-time, she had to babysit a lot and virtually raised her siblings. The end result was that she had a bit more maturity than the rest of us, and we all tried our best not to hold that against her when she made us feel stupid.

Crisco loved popular music, was a good athlete, and prided herself on keeping up with the boys in all our childhood adventures. For our part, we all pretty much fell over each other competing for her affection or favor—and she ate that up like biscuits and gravy on Sunday morning! One of my first recollections of popular music was Crisco dancing to Chubby Checker's 1961 hit song **"Let's Twist Again,"** and making us all take turns learning how to twist with her. That was quite a sight: all those young, uncoordinated boys twisting out in the front yard, trying to impress the girl "with all that!" Besides her looks and personality, Crisco was street smart. She was an asset to planning our adventures in a way that added some common sense. This would come in handy as time progressed.

Just as Crisco walked up, David "Crazy Ike" Eichenmuller, or sometimes just "Ike," pulled up on his 1974 Honda CR125M Elsinore. He and Goondoggy had bought their bikes together as a package deal to get a better price, and those were the two hottest bikes in our group. Crazy Ike was the product of a big German father and a demure Irish mother, large for his age but not heavy. He was covered head to toe with freckles. Ike could never seem to look my mother in the eye when he came to our house, so when we were little kids, she told me I was not to hang out with him, which basically ensured that Crazy Ike and I would spend plenty of time together.

Crazy Ike was two years older than the rest of us. He could be a bit of a troublemaker, and was somewhat unique in the various skill sets of our Bad Love gang. He could steal anything at any time, and either get away with it or lie his way out of it. He was one of those people who really didn't obey the rules or laws, and somehow never seemed to get caught. Watching Ike in action was sometimes a bit like watching the devil at work knowing he was on your side; you liked the results, but you tried to somehow ignore or forget the methods. As an example, as a young teenager, he worked at a sporting goods store. Everyone loved him there because he was so brutally cynical; he cursed like a sailor, and made everyone laugh at mundane events. None of us had money, but we would need gear for our camping trips. Crazy Ike would take our orders of what gear we needed for our trips, then have us purchase a large cooler from the sporting goods store and tell us to pick it up at the loading dock. We would pick up the cooler at the dock in its packing box and note that it seemed heavy. He'd say, "Oh, that's just some of those damn ice packs weighing it down." When we opened the box and raised the cooler lid at home, there was everything we had listed!

Crazy Ike was the first of us to turn sixteen, and he got his driver's license on his birthday. He loved loud rock music and driving fast, but had little money—so his first car was a piece of shit, 1965 American Motors Rambler that he bought for $100. It had over 100,000 miles on it at the time. The body was rusting, the seats were torn and stained, and it had a grossly anemic 6-cylinder engine that dripped and burned oil—but it ran! With Willy's expert help, Ike fitted it with the latest 8-track tape deck and great rear-deck speakers. He wanted to be able to burn rubber in that car so badly that he had all of us pick up the rear end while he slammed the pedal to the floor in drive, then we dropped it to the concrete. It made a little squeal, punctuated with a puff of tire smoke, and Crazy Ike was on cloud nine! It was amazing that the transmission survived that maneuver. We drove everywhere in that car, and you could hear us coming from a mile away with the Beatles, Creedence Clearwater Revival, or Alice Cooper blasting away on 8-track tapes.

Crazy Ike pulled up to the rest of us like a wild man and laid down a skid mark ten feet long on the street in front of my house. He turned off his engine and challenged us, "Any of you panty-waisted boys wanna go for a *real* ride today?"

I promptly responded, "You know, Ike, you are like one of those things that we don't appreciate enough until it's gone...like toilet paper. So come on over here and kiss my ass, buttercup!" The whole group about died laughing.

Ike replied, "I'll get you for that later today, BB, but I talked to Waldo before I came over here, and the Pud, Meatball, Tater, and Spaghetti Head are all over at Waldo's house or headed there, and will wait there for us to go take a ride. The Runt is the one we are waiting for to get here."

Donny "The Runt" Legrande, a French-American kid, was a year older than me and a year younger than Crazy Ike. Legrande got his nickname because he was at a minimum a foot shorter than the least of us, and stayed that way as we all grew up. He despised that nickname, but we were consistently "gracious" with all the names we gave out. Donny was the son of a lifelong aircraft mechanic, Bud Legrande, who quite literally had every tool known to man neatly arranged in his self-designed, very large, garage and workshop. Bud not only knew everything about fixing aircraft engines, he could fix cars, boats, lawnmowers...you name it, so long as it ran on gasoline, diesel, or aviation fuel. As a result, Donny grew up living, breathing, eating, and consuming everything as it related to working on internal combustion engines. He could troubleshoot and fix just about anything mechanical, and certainly anything that ran on gasoline. His skill set would certainly come in handy later when we discovered time travel.

The Runt was short, but he was a very fast sprinter, could turn on a dime (or less), and jump fences like they weren't there. He was like a Chihuahua that loved to pick on all the bigger dogs. He would routinely taunt Crazy Ike or Goondoggy by kicking them in the ass and then daring them to try and catch him. It was hilarious fun, watching the Runt outmaneuver anyone trying to catch him; they rarely could even lay a finger on him, but they made sure to flip him off as he ran away.

The Runt was equally resourceful when it came to getting away from trouble during our various childhood adventures. When our Bad Love Gang was in the range of twelve to thirteen years old, we all had smaller mini-bikes and Honda Mini Trail 70s. As you might expect, Donny and his dad, Bud, built his mini-bike totally from scratch; it was basically a few steel tubes wrapped around the largest Briggs and Stratton motor they could find, giving it a very high power-to-weight ratio. It was more geared for hill-climbing power than overall speed. All of us could do a good 40–45 MPH on our bikes, but the Runt's bike topped out at about 35 MPH. One weekend we were "permanently borrowing" some lumber and nails from an apartment complex under construction, planning to use them for our latest treehouse project in the woods. The building superintendent was unexpectedly there that weekend, and came after us in an old beat-up pickup truck. The Runt and Willy were riding together on the Runt's mini-bike and the superintendent was gaining on them as the rest of us cleanly got away. Knowing that they were too close for comfort and about to be caught, the Runt reached down with one hand and disengaged the governor mechanism from that big Briggs and Stratton motor. We all then witnessed a childhood miracle; the Runt's mini-bike lurched forward and took off like a bolt of lightning, leaving that crappy old pickup truck in its dust. The Runt was our hero that day, and none of us ever forgot the sight of that escape! It became part of the lore of our Bad Love Club experience.

Three minutes after Crazy Ike arrived, the Runt pulled up on his 1973 Honda SL 100. It was almost to be expected that he would be the last to arrive, as he had that reputation with the Bad Love Gang. True to form, he rode up to us, looked around, and said, "What the hell took you guys so long? Let's get out of here!" With that, Crisco jumped on the back of Willy's bike, Bowmar rode on the back of my bike, and we all took off for Waldo's house to rendezvous with the rest of the group, then head out for our Sunday ride.

CHAPTER FIVE

THE BAD LOVE GANG STUMBLES ONTO DESTINY

"There's nowhere you can be that isn't
where you're meant to be..."
—John Lennon

W e all rode straight to Paul "Waldo" Thompson's house, which was only a few blocks away in our neighborhood. Waldo and his wife, Mary, were in their early forties and for unspoken reasons, were not able to have children of their own. As we were all growing up, Waldo and Mary "adopted" the entire Bad Love Gang and served as secondary, surrogate parents to all of us. Their house was always open to us; we spent a lot of time there playing cards, talking about every life topic under the sun, and watching TV shows together. We regularly watched *Mash*, *The Six Million Dollar Man*, and we especially loved the paranormal *Kolchak: The Night Stalker*. Waldo was a Korean War army veteran, and worked in procurement at the Oak Ridge National Laboratory. Mary worked as a law clerk for the Knoxville court system. They both loved to camp, and had a 1973 Airstream Safari Land Yacht 23 parked in their expanded driveway. Both Waldo and Mary knew how to handle firearms, and Waldo had quite a gun collection of pistols, shotguns, and rifles. Waldo routinely went on camping and canoe float trips with all of us and was an honorary member of the Bad Love

Gang. At age 42 in June of 1974, he was nearly bald and that somehow earned him the nickname Waldo, as opposed to "Baldo." Mary was such an incredibly nice and sweet woman that we never made the effort to assign her a nickname, although we frequently joked about how on earth Waldo managed to marry such a great woman.

As we all arrived at Waldo's house, Gary "the Pud" Jacobson and Frankie "Spaghetti Head" Russo were both standing in the driveway talking to Waldo and Mary. The Pud got his nickname from being average at every sporting event we played as kids. He would get the awards for attendance. In reality, he was quite resourceful and depend-able at any job assigned to him, and I always knew that I could rely on him in a pinch. He was excellent at using walkie-talkies and various wireless communication devices available in the early 1970s. The Pud was also great at doing tedious or time-consuming jobs, and this would be important in his upcoming time travel assignment. He rode a ruby red, Honda SL 90 that was only produced for one year: 1969.

Frankie "Spaghetti Head" Russo, standing next to the Pud, was from a large, Italian Catholic family that had recently moved to the neighborhood. He was the newest member of the Bad Love Gang. Frankie did not yet own a motorcycle or dirt bike, but he did like to go riding with us. Frankie got his nickname because of his big Italian family and his incredibly thick, curly hair, which looked like someone had dumped a bowl of spaghetti upside down on top of his head. He added a Mafia-style touch to our gang, and we always enjoyed his various Italian descriptions of things during our adventures.

A few minutes after we all said hi in Waldo's driveway, Meatball and Tater arrived together on Tater's 1974 Harley Davidson SX 125. Danny "Tater" Ford had the only non-Honda bike in our entire gang, and he was a southern boy to his core. Tater had grown up in a military family in Columbus, Georgia and moved to Oak Ridge when he was about seven or eight years old. Danny served as our gang's continual, nonstop source of Southern-fried humor. There was no telling what he would say or come up with next, but he always had something to say that made us all laugh.

Aaron "Meatball" Eisen came from a Jewish family, and he was a jack of all trades. Meatball could fix anything mechanical or electric that the Runt wouldn't or couldn't tackle. Meatball had a true heart of gold and was always ready to lend a hand and help anyone at any time. His Jewish background and upbringing would add a valuable dimension and deeper meaning to the focus of our soon-to-be-discovered secret of the century and time travel mission.

Once Tater and Meatball had arrived at Waldo's house, the Bad Love Gang was all there—except for Bowmar's sister, Cleopatra. She had been out late the night before, and had slept in that morning. I looked at everyone and said, "How about we take a ride west and south over toward the river near the K-25 site? There are some good trails with dips and hills to give us all a challenge or two."

Tater jumped in and said, "Didn't we just cover that ground the other day?"

I replied, "No Tater, we haven't been over there for at least a couple months."

Tater fired back in his thickest southern accent, "When I say 'the other day,' it can mean anytime from yesterday to three hundred sixty-four days ago! Whatever we're gonna do, let's do it fast; it's getting hot out here, and I'm starting to sweat like a whore in church!" We all busted out laughing, then said goodbye to Waldo and Mary and headed out for a ride in the woods and trails located west and south of town. It was quite a symphony of motorcycle notes as we pulled away from Waldo's house on a beautiful Sunday in June morning for a ride.

There was a significant backdrop of history regarding the location of our Sunday morning ride on June 9, 1974. On September 19, 1942, General Leslie Groves was chosen by President Franklin Roosevelt to oversee the Manhattan Project. General Groves subsequently selected 59,000 acres of land along the Clinch River, about twenty miles west of Knoxville, as the site that would be tasked to learn how best to enrich the uranium that would make the world's first atomic bomb. In September 1942, the area was very rural and ideal for a project that needed to be kept top secret. It wasn't called Oak Ridge then, but referred to as Site X, or the Clinton Engineering Works, CEW for short. Eleven miles southwest of the original headquarters at Oak Ridge on the Clinch River was the site chosen for the K-25 plant for uranium enrichment. The mile-long, U-shaped K-25 plant covered forty-four acres, was four stories high, and up to 400 feet wide. Engineers had developed special coatings for hundreds of miles of pipes and equipment at K-25 to withstand the corrosive uranium hexafluoride gas that would pass through the plant. The entire process was hermetically sealed like a thermos bottle, since any leakage of moisture could cause a violent reaction with the uranium hexafluoride. Innovative foundation techniques were required and at one time, it was the largest building in the world under one roof. The simultaneous undertaking of the adjacent, equally demanding, and even more secretive White Hole Project went virtually unnoticed in the midst of this incredibly massive, top-secret construction project in rural Tennessee. Just like so many times before, we were headed in the direction of the Clinch River near this area to have some fun for the day. This particular Sunday would be different.

There were a lot of backwoods trails in this area. The K-25 site, which borders the Clinch River, occupied about 1,300 acres with more than half of it still closed off by security fences. There were numerous old, dirt country roads and paths great for dirt biking fun; we were riding on the eastern and southern fringes of the K-25 acreage, but didn't go all the way down to the river. There are some interesting ravines where water probably collects and flows to the Clinch river after heavy rains, and we loved to challenge each other to ride down one steep side of those ravines and then up the steep other side. As we approached one particularly challenging ravine a bit off our usual beaten path, it appeared to originate from a small hillside where a couple of pine trees had fallen down at the mouth or start of the ravine. Crazy Ike and Goondoggy saw it first, and waved everyone else on to take a look. This one wasn't nearly as deep a V as some of our craziest challenges, but it was a fairly steep climb up the opposite side. I knew that I could make it alone, but having Bowmar on the back would make it very difficult. Crazy Ike went first and spun his rear tire excessively on the other side, but made it over the top. Goon-doggy went second, taking it faster down, and made it up the other side smoothly. I yelled over to ask if they thought Bowmar and I could make it together. Crazy Ike yelled back, "You can't make by yourself, Bubble Shit, much less with Bowmar Brainiac on that bike with you!"

Bowmar said to me, "BB, even if we don't make it and come back down into the ravine, I can jump off and get away freely so long as you can do what you need to do. It looks like a pretty soft landing zone at the bottom of this ravine, so long as you stay close to the mouth and away from those fallen trees." That is why I loved Bowmar so much; he had already calculated the best approach and the worst-case scenario!

I yelled back at Crazy Ike, "If Bowmar and I make it, then you grill the burgers tonight. If we don't make it, then we do the grilling."

Ike responded, "You're on, Bubble Nuts!" He then whispered to Goondoggy, "I'll make sure they do the cooking tonight." Everyone was watching from both sides as we made our descent into the ravine. I stood on my foot pegs and told Bowmar to lean forward and push himself forward from his rear, buddy foot pegs. We came down quick and started up the other side with reasonably good momentum. As we got closer to the top of the other side, I gunned the throttle and the rear tire began to spin and throw dirt wildly out behind us. I thought I could hear the guys behind us cheering for us, and indeed Meatball was screaming, "Go, you son of a bitch!" at the top of his lungs. We had just enough momentum and traction to crest the top of the hill with our front tire–but the rear tire was still spinning, digging in and throwing dirt. We might have made it or jumped off at the top of the other side, but then Crazy Ike pulled a fast one. He positioned his bike in front of us as we were cresting the top edge of the ravine, then got low and spun a donut, spewing dirt and debris at us. I blinked and let off the throttle for just a second too long, at precisely the wrong time. Even though I hit the throttle again immediately, I could feel us sliding backwards. I yelled at Bowmar to jump and bail out; as soon as I could sense that Bowmar was off the bike, I then laid the bike to its side and simultaneously jumped free as well. The bike, Bowmar, and I all slid to the bottom of the ravine, and I managed to slide feet first and keep one hand on the handle grip of the bike. Fortunately, Bowmar stayed clear of the bike and we found ourselves at the bottom of the ravine, laughing that we were still in one piece and cursing at Ike at the same time. We reassured everyone that both we and the bike had survived the slide down intact.

It was then that destiny struck.

Bowmar was staring up the ravine toward the small hillside where it originated. He said, "BB, look at that doorway cracked open in the hillside." What we could never have seen from the top of either side of the ravine was obvious from our vantage point at the bottom, gazing up from under the two fallen trees spanning the ravine. There was a concrete tunnel opening with a doorway that must have been hidden for a long time. The concrete appeared cracked, as if it had been damaged in an earthquake. I asked Bowmar, "When was our last significant earthquake?"

As far as earthquakes go, Eastern Tennessee is on shaky ground. The region experiences more seismic activity than just about anywhere else in the eastern United States. Bowmar, with his genius IQ, naturally remembers just about everything that happens and immediately replied, "Less than eight months ago; on October thirtieth, 1973, a four point seven-magnitude quake rocked this area."

"That's right, there was some damage in Knoxville from that quake," I mused.

Bowmar continued, "Yes, and more than thirty aftershocks occurred south of Knoxville during the latter part of last year. It was the strongest earthquake since the five point nine that hit Knoxville in 1913. Maybe that quake last fall cracked that tunnel open and knocked down those two pine trees as well."

"How about you and I go for a little adventure and see where that tunnel leads?" I suggested.

Bowmar responded, "You lead the way, Sherlock, and I'll be right behind you."

I then yelled up to the group, "Anyone got a good flashlight? Bowmar and I found a tunnel opening down here, and we want to check it out." Meatball and the Runt, who were both always prepared for disaster to strike, each tossed down a flashlight. I told the rest of them to go have fun, and we would catch up with them in a little while.

Bowmar and I dusted ourselves off and made our way over to the open tunnel entrance. The doorway was major league thick, obviously built to keep people out and protect what was contained within. The hatchway was open just wide enough for us to squeeze by and gain entrance. The tunnel was completely dry; it was of all concrete construction, with some small cracks visible in the walls and floor, but fully intact. It definitely did not appear to be a large sewage or drainage pipe. It seemed to be some sort of underground walkway leading to the damaged exit. We turned and headed into the tunnel, and it soon became apparent that we were walking on a gradual downward slope. I stopped and pointed this out to Bowmar, "You do realize that we are walking downhill in this tunnel. That means it is not for any kind of drainage, because water would be flowing in the direction we are heading. In addition, I have noticed some drainage vents spaced along the floor against the walls."

Bowmar smiled and replied, "Of course Mr. Holmes, your powers of deduction are keenly aware of our surroundings and that gives me great comfort!"

I responded, "Mind your P's and Q's, Watson, we are on to something big!"

We continued walking for what seemed to be a bit further than a quarter of a mile, occasionally knocking down cobwebs as we went—but overall, the tunnel was surprisingly clean. Whoever constructed it knew what they were doing. We came to the end of the tunnel and saw that there was a very large door, held shut by a wheel latch like you might see on a submarine. It took both of us to get the wheel turning to unlock the door. Once open, there was another twenty feet of hallway that opened into what appeared to be a much larger, pitch-black room. We were not ready to experience the magnitude or depth of the space we were about to enter, but above that entrance, for the first time in my life, I saw a sign with the phrase *THE WHITE HOLE*. My heart jumped in my chest and time stood still; my life would never be the same again.

CHAPTER SIX
THE TIME MACHINE

T he entrance to the gigantic and cavernous time machine room, or "the vault," as we came to call it, had a sign above it that Bowmar and I stopped and carefully reviewed using our flashlights to see. The sign read as follows:

THE WHITE HOLE
"People who believe in physics, know that the
distinction between past, present and future
is only a stubbornly persistent illusion."
—Albert Einstein

"Courage is not the absence of fear, but
rather the assessment that something else
is more important than fear."
—Franklin D. Roosevelt

Once through the entrance, we found an impressive power lever on our right and switched it to the *on* position. The lights instantly jumped to life and lit the entire vault brightly. The vault was cylindrical in shape, larger than anything either of us could have imagined. Its contents were at once both marvelous and breathtaking. We were visually and physically stunned as we surveyed the space around us, and I found myself covered in goose bumps and temporarily speechless. All of this incredible space was well below ground, with mature hardwoods and evergreen forest growing above it. Bowmar was the first to speak. He looked at me, basically in a state of hyperventilation and nervously declared, "BB, we just walked into the holy grail of physics! I must have just died and gone to heaven!" His voice was very high-pitched, almost as if he'd been inhaling helium.

I replied, "No Bowmar, you have not assumed room temperature just yet. We are *well* below ground, and this is really happening!"

The level of our entrance was at the middle or 3rd floor of the vault, also designated as year *1943*. There were five floors total, and two large circular "racetrack" machines: one high above us at the fifth floor, which was also designated as the year *1945*, and one at the ground floor that appeared to be the centerpiece of the machine's functionality. The upper racetrack machine was noticeably larger in diameter than the lower. Interestingly, the ground floor was also designated as NOW rather than a specific year.

The central core of the vault was open from floor to ceiling so that the upper racetrack machine was free to move up and down from the second floor to the fifth floor, where it was currently parked. The upper racetrack was mounted on huge vertical runners, calibrated with deep notches so that it could be moved like an elevator with high precision to position the upper machine up and down the circular vault to years *1942*, *1943*, *1944*, or *1945*. The upper racetrack could be positioned at any day during each of those 4 designated years using the calibrated runners; it became apparent that each notch represented a day in that year.

The walls on each of the five floors were lined with 1940s-era computers, all standing about ten feet tall with various dials, meters, gauges, warning lights, and switches that were truly the stuff of 1940's science fiction. Later on, Bowmar and I would discover that each year's floor had three identical, parallel backup systems to function as successive failsafes in the event that any one or two failed for any reason. America's space-age approach to exotic technology and backing up that technology to ensure mission safety and integrity had started during World War II. The lower circular racetrack was located in the center of the ground floor; the center of that racetrack was a type of a circular stage that looked sort of like a comfy-cozy sunken living room. The space was covered in soft cushions, with seating for more than a dozen people. Very weird!

Hovering above the center of the ground floor was a large funnel-shaped tube with one wide opening that matched the larger diameter of the upper racetrack, and a narrower but still wide central telescopic tube that matched the diameter of the circular ground floor stage. I took notice of several sealed ports along the narrower central telescopic tube, each marked with the words EXOTIC MATTER. The lower end of the funnel tube ended in a reverse wide-mouthed opening that matched the smaller diameter of the ground floor racetrack. The lower opening of the funnel tube was uniquely different because it was transparent. It appeared that upper and lower openings of the telescopic funnel tube could be docked with the upper and lower racetracks, respectively. From our vantage point, even when docked to the lower racetrack, you would be able to see through the transparent lower funnel opening, and see what was happening in the center of the lower racetrack. Already, Bowmar and I were beginning to sense how this might potentially function (or was purposed to function). Shivers of excitement and fear ran down my spine and my goosebumps came back with a vengeance.

t had been a long time since it was opened; it again
us to get the heavy steel door open. Bowmar looked at
asked, "Do you think that we are authorized to enter?"
, "In the words of Henry David Thoreau 'Any fool can
d any fool will mind it.' So follow me, Bowmar." We
m and turned on the lights. It appeared to be a large
sorts, with various instruments, spectrometers, Geiger
ts & measures, microscopes, you name it.

d through the lab towards the back of the room, we
er office with windows situated to view out into the
o the office and stacked against the back wall, there
crates that were all labeled *Top Secret*. These were even
g because each cube was about one square foot in size,
ll stacked, numbered, and dated very neatly. We went
and began systematically searching the desk and the
hind the desk. Everything was in its place as if nothing
ned, and the next work day was ready to get started. It
ching, but I found what appeared to be a log book.

d I read through it together. The log book detailed the
xotic matter, which had been obtained from an alien
had crashed at Indian Springs Airfield, AKA Groom
he southwest Nevada desert in June of 1942. The log
tained details on each serial numbered crate of exotic
nen each of those crates had been delivered to the lab.
to be delivered was checked in on Tuesday, April 10,
, looked at me and said, "President Franklin D. Roo-
a massive stroke in the afternoon of Thursday, April
5."

Bowmar and asked, "How on earth do you remember
that?!"

We then moved away from the entrance, walked around the perimeter of the third floor, and came to a set of double doors with signage above that read:

MEDICAL BAY
"A ship is always safe at shore,
but that is not what it is built for."
—Albert Einstein

The inside of the medical bay had two operating tables with large overhead lights. The walls were lined with white metal cabinets, glass doors revealing that the cabinets were fully stocked with medical supplies such as gloves, syringes, scalpels, suture material, etc. We noticed that one of the cabinets was marked *Implantable GCPDs*; the shelves inside were filled with these GCPDs, which were curiously packaged in numbered boxes of matching pairs. The GCPDs were spherical, shiny metal objects about the diameter of a small cherry tomato or American quarter. The boxes containing the GCPDs were labelled *First device to be implanted in the cheek of the buttocks using sterile technique, and matching device inserted in control panel prior to launch or recall*. Bowmar and I would soon discover that GCPD stood for global cosmic positioning device.

Down the hall from the Medical Bay was another set of double doors.

WARDROBE WAREHOUSE
"Courage is being scared to death...
and saddling up anyway."
—John Wayne

"Whenever I am faced with two evils,
I take the one I haven't tried before."
—Mae West

We went through the doors and to our amazement, it was a huge room with sections and rows upon rows of clothing that seemed endless. The male and female clothing was essentially arranged by nation and region, and also by World War II Army, Navy, Marine and Air Force—military forces including the United States, Britain, Australia, China, Germany, Italy, Japan, etc. In addition, there were shoes, belts, boots, medals, insignia, and rank appliques for each branch. Even more amazing, there was a small arms/firearms section correlating with each of the WWII military forces. There was civilian clothing too, for what seemed like every country or region on earth, and no detail was left out; there were coats, gloves, hats, and other accessories galore! The wardrobe warehouse alone was worth a fortune, and would leave anyone from Hollywood drooling and green with envy.

Bowmar and I then made our way down to the ground floor level marked *NOW*. There was an impressive control panel area in front of the lower racetrack machine, with command and control functions that seemed clearly marked. There were *power* levers for the upper and lower racetrack machines; switches marked *lower dock* and *upper dock*, presumably for the telescopic, central connector funnel; and large command buttons marked *SEND* and *RECALL*. One section of the control panel was dedicated to programing a specific global geographic location using precise coordinates of latitude, longitude, and elevation. There was also a separate section for docking and locking up to fifteen of the global cosmic positioning devices (GCPDs) in place. Bowmar and I collectively surmised that the machine could send up to a maximum of fifteen souls to the years 1942, 1943, 1944, or 1945, and then recall them back to the present time.

We then walked through
lower racetrack machine and i
track. This was the area that ha
living room covered in soft cus
floor above. Not only was it trul
it also had a trampoline-like fl
that the time travelers returnin
tunnel might be falling back ont
Bowmar and I jumped up and
stage like a couple of little kids

"I know where I'm gonna
hours in this place. Speaking of
dinosaur, Bowman?"

Bowmar responded, "Beats n
I replied, "A dino*snore!*"

Bowmar smiled, shook his h
of your all-time worst jokes, BB.
back to the stone ages for that or

We then left the lower racetra
and into the circular ground fl
the other side, opposite the con
doorway. This one was a huge s
airlock-type latch. Above this door

EXOTIC MATTE
AUTHORIZED P
"A new type of thinking
survive and move t
—Alber

Obviously,
took the two o
me, smiled and

I responded
make a rule an
entered the ro
research lab of
counters, weig

As we mov
saw a rear cor
lab. Adjacent
were heavy-du
more interesti
and they were
into the office
bookshelves b
had ever happ
took some sea

Bowmar a
origin of the
spaceship tha
Dry Lake, in
book also cor
matter, and w
The last crate
1945. Bowma
sevelt died of
twelfth of 194

I stared a
something lik

"I can't help it; that's the way my memory works. But I bet that this place getting shut down and sealed off was somehow connected to FDR's sudden death."

From that day forward, Bowmar and I swore each other to secrecy about our discovery. We set out to learn about the secrets of the white hole and this marvelous time machine, how it worked, and what we would do with this life-changing discovery. Somebody had spent a spectacular fortune, in both money and effort, to make this White Hole Project a reality. And here it sat, like it was ready to fire up and use, but somehow the project got lost in time.

CHAPTER SEVEN
TIME TRAVEL IS BOTH REAL AND POSSIBLE

"I am thankful for all those who said NO to me.
It's because of them I'm doing it myself."
—Albert Einstein

B owmar and I began to research time travel like there was no tomor-row. The other Bad Love Gang members were both curious and suspicious of what we were up to, and wanted to know why we were spending so much time together. At every opportunity, I let the Bad Love Gang know that we had a great surprise coming their way, one that would "blow their socks off and set their hair on fire!" I calmly and confidently told our gang that our biggest adventure ever was coming soon. It was fun to have a new secret that all of them were lusting to know.

Early in our research efforts, Bowmar and I would have some rather deep discussions regarding the nature of time on many levels. While I came from a rather religious family, Bowmar was agnostic (a doubter of God's existence) and his family trended more toward atheism. One night during our "time studies" in the midst of snacking on popcorn, pretzels, Reese's peanut butter cups, and Coca Cola while we listened to a stack of 45 RPM vinyl records playing on my parents' Magnavox Console Stereo, I asked Bowmar to humor me for a moment as I ultimately brought God into the equation. "So Bowmar, I am reading about the work of a German physicist, Kurt Godel, who described reality as consisting of an infinite number of layers of 'now,' which come into existence one after the other or in succession. Any person or observer of one layer has his or her own set of 'nows,' and cannot claim that their layer of time or 'now' has priority over another, different layer of time. In other words..." I walk over to the stereo, which is eerily and conveniently playing **"In the Year 2525"** by Zagar and Evans... "time is like this stack of records: Each record could represent a year, and you can go back and replay that year whenever you want. It always plays the same way, time after time, and it is always there ready to play when you go to it."

Bowmar responded just as the next song began to play: **"Incense and Peppermints"** by Strawberry Alarm Clock. "Maybe in some way that partially explains the circular racetracks of our time machine, but just know that I'm not giving you any new 'discovery credits' for making comparisons to your record collection, Buzzard Butt! So, what does God have to do with this discussion?"

I answered, "OK, so just for a minute, imagine that God is real and you have died and gone to heaven. God wants to show you some things about your life and take you back in time. You, Bowmar, are going back to your earlier life in the 1960s, or now in the early 70s. But what if you were from the 1800s, or the 1400s? God would take you back to your life at that time of recorded history. Everything and everyone would be there, in its place, just as it was during your life. God created time just like everything else that has come or will come into existence: past, present, and future. Time is real and time travel is real; we just have to unlock the secrets of God as created in physics, and learn how to travel to any layer of time and back."

Bowmar replied, "That's cool, BB, but I still have my doubts about the God part of all that." As Bowmar finished, **"I Can See Clearly Now"** by Johnny Nash was the next song to play.

We collected time travel research papers in droves, read them avidly, and then discussed how all those theories applied to the time machine in the White Hole Project vault. As it turns out, an Austrian physicist named Ludwig Flamm was the first to coin the phrase *white hole* in 1916, while reviewing Einstein's theory of general relativity. He surmised that a white hole could be a theoretical time reversal of a black hole, and that entrances to both black and white holes could be connected by a spacetime conduit. We surmised that we had now found the origin of the name for the White Hole Project.

In 1935 (29 years after Flamm coined the phrase *white hole*), using Einstein's theory of relativity, Einstein and physicist Nathan Rosen proposed the existence of spacetime bridges that could connect two different points in spacetime. These bridges could theoretically create a virtual shortcut that could reduce travel time and distance through space. These virtual shortcuts came to be called Einstein-Rosen bridges. In the 1960s, the physicist John Wheeler named these bridges or connections wormholes, imagining a worm taking a shortcut through an apple rather than going around the apple. Einstein's theory of general relativity mathematically predicted the presence of wormholes that would have two funnel openings, or mouths, connected by a neck (like our time travel machine). Our research showed that for a wormhole (or in our time machine's case, a white hole) to be functioning as a time machine, it would require stability or it could quickly collapse. The solution to this inherent instability would require some very exotic matter to keep the white hole open and immutable for a long enough span of time to travel through time and then return back to the present. Although exotic matter was not known to exist on earth, the White Hole Project developers had gotten their hands on enough exotic matter to make time travel feasible. The bluish material found oozing from the breaches in the hull of the alien spaceship that crashed in Area 51 in June of 1942 had opened some of the secrets of spacetime travel, allowing for the creation of a wormhole (or white hole) that was stable enough for time travel to actually occur.

Assuming that the funnel tube connecting the lower and upper racetracks was lined with exotic matter to keep the white hole open and traversable, Bowmar began to surmise how this time machine might work. "So, Bubble Brain...oh, I mean Bubble *Butt*..."

I responded, "Very funny, 'Be...low me'... Oh, I mean "Bowmar."

Bowmar continued, "One aspect of Einstein's theory of relativity is known as the phenomenon of time dilation. We would need to speed up the side of the large mouth of the exotic matter-lined funnel close to the speed of light, while leaving the smaller mouth side at a stationary or slower fixed speed. According to the theory or phenomenon of time dilation, time in the proximity of the near light-speed mouth will slow down significantly, relative to the stationary or slower, fixed-speed, smaller mouth. Therefore, for example, if the fixed mouth ages thirty years, the high-speed mouth ages only one year. A time traveler entering the fixed speed mouth in 1974 would emerge through the near light speed mouth in 1944. It's the exotic matter keeping the neck of the funnel open during the time travel process that makes the connection possible. I think in our case that the larger racetrack is accelerating matter close to the speed of light and it gets positioned exactly to the year and day of time that we are traveling back to."

I actually grasped the concept and said, "Now that makes you, Bowmar, a steely-eyed missile man!"

We spent untold hours during the summer of 1974 working at the White Hole Project site and learning how to use the equipment. While researching various events of World War II, I happened upon the unbelievable story of the Phantom Fortress, and kept coming across stories of the Holocaust as well. The more that I read about the Holocaust, the more it haunted me. One night while all of these things were fresh on my mind, I had a dream about the Bad Love Gang flying the B-17 Phantom Fortress. We were coming through the clouds on a beautiful moonlit night...and then I woke up. My brain was connecting various dots, and that night I shared an idea for a time travel rescue mission with Bowmar. Sometimes ideas and things in life just fall into place; usually those are the things that are meant to be. Bowmar loved my plan; we then did the necessary research to create a time travel mission that the Bad Love Gang could proudly undertake.

CHAPTER EIGHT

MISSION PLANNING

"If you aim at nothing, you will hit it every time."
—Zig Ziglar

Wednesday, August 7th, 1974, 5:00 PM,
Waldo and Mary Thompson's home in Oak Ridge, Tennessee

One thing about Paul "Waldo" and Mary Thompson, no matter what, your secrets were sacred with them. It had been nearly two full months since Bowmar and I had stumbled onto destiny and discovered the White Hole Project. After our amazing discovery on that fateful day of June 9th, we had told the Bad Love Gang that the tunnel we found was an old extra or backup drainage pipe coming from K-25. No one had given it a second thought. However, the group did know that Bowmar and I had been vigorously planning some kind of new, big adventure; they just never could have imagined how big!

A few weeks prior to this night, Bowmar and I had spent an evening with Waldo and Mary, giving them the details of our discovery of the White Hole Project—and telling them that we fully believed time travel was real and possible. We explained that we were working on a time travel mission for the Bad Love Gang, and needed to get everyone together in one place to reveal what we were planning. It only made sense that we make this announcement at their house in the middle of the week (when everyone could attend) using the irresistible entice-ment of "burgers, brats, and pork and beans at Waldo's place." The four of us had made certain that everyone had been contacted at least twice and had RSVP'd that they were coming tonight. Everyone in the Bad Love Gang to a person had RSVP'd in the affirmative, and Bowmar and I were totally prepared to make our case to the group and hand out mission assignments. We had a little over three months before the mission we had planned would take place; the dates to make this particular mission successful were "hard" dates, and could not be changed. Making this certifiably crazy paranormal mission plan believable to the group had required considerable forethought. Having Waldo and Mary both on board beforehand would also provide some needed credibility.

The entire gang came as planned, and we were all joking around as our usual selves as we grilled burgers and brats. When dinner had been served, Waldo loudly announced that he and Mary had some-thing important to tell everyone over dinner. He asked everyone to come into their great room with their food. As a group, we typically sat in their great room watching TV shows together; in fact, the TV was loudly playing the Wednesday Evening News as we were all sitting down.

We all looked at the TV with astonishment and amazement, as the newscast was showing a man walking a high wire—a *very* high wire. That very morning of August 7, 1974, Philippe Petit, a 24-year-old French high-wire artist, had gained worldwide fame for his walk on a wire stretched between the roofs of the Twin Towers of the World Trade Center in Manhattan, a quarter mile above the ground. The towers were still under construction at that time. He performed for roughly 45 minutes, making eight passes along the wire, during which he walked, danced, lay down on the wire, and even saluted watchers from a kneeling position. The people on the streets of New York far below—office workers, construction crews, and policemen, mostly—all cheered him on. This was the perfect segue for me and Bowmar to make our Bad Love Gang time travel mission announcement to the group.

Waldo turned off the TV set and got started. "The only thing that Mary and I really have to say at this moment is to tell all of you to look and listen very carefully to what BB and Bowmar have to show and tell you tonight. They shared this secret with the two of us weeks ago, and since then, I have personally inspected the actual site that you are about to see in photographs. You all know that I am a Korean War veteran with a sizable gun collection." Waldo smiled, looking at the other members of our group. "You take the secret you are about to hear tonight to your graves many, many years from now, so that my friends Smith and Wesson don't have to accelerate that process for you!"

Tater spoke up in his heavy southern accent. "This sounds like something that'll make yer liver quiver and yer bladder splatter!" Everyone laughed at that ice-breaker. Tater then asked, "Are you going on this new, super-secret mission with us there, Colonel Waldo?"

Waldo replied, "As a matter of fact, I *am* going on this particular mission. And y'all will be calling me '*General* Waldo,' thank you very much!"

I stood up and took the floor. "Ladies and gentleman—and I use that phrase very loosely—the mission plan and adventure that we are going to share with you tonight will make that high-wire act we just saw on TV look like a Sunday stroll in the park! Remember that day back in June, when we took the ride out by the old K-25 property?"

"Yeah...the day my donut spin-out spoiled yours and Bowmar's shot at glory at the top of that ravine?" Crazy Ike chimed in.

I replied, "Yep, that was the day. And you, Crazy Ike, actually led us to more glory than anyone could ever imagine! That tunnel opening that we found that day was not a backup drainage pipe for K-25; it was an alternate entrance for a top-secret World War II project called the White Hole Project. Before I explain further, Bowmar and I want you to look at these pictures, so you don't think that this is an elaborate prank or joke. We took these pictures of the White Hole Project with my Dad's Polaroid SX-70 camera so that there would be no trace, no negatives lingering somewhere for anyone else to see these pictures." Bowmar distributed ten pictures that circulated amongst the group, showing various perspectives of the White Hole Project's time travel machine.

After everyone had seen the pictures, Bowmar spoke up. "I know it sounds radical, but this White Hole Project is a time travel machine that was designed as a backup plan to the Manhattan Project." Being from Oak Ridge all of us knew about the Manhattan Project, and had since we were very young. "If Hitler and the Nazis had gotten the atomic bomb first, we, the USA, were going to use this machine to go back in time in an effort to stop the Nazis. The Manhattan Project succeeded; the U.S. got the atomic bomb first, and we used it to end World War II. For reasons still not entirely clear, the White Hole Project got sealed off in secrecy, and has remained a secret to this day. It appears to have somehow ended abruptly about the time President Roosevelt died. Everything there is like new, in mint condition and just a little dusty. It is still connected to the power grid, and is ready to use as soon as we are ready to use it. The time machine is designed to carry up to fifteen people back in time to any day or place on earth during the WWII global war years, between 1942 and 45, and then bring them back in time to now. Bubble Butt and I are proposing a type of rescue mission on a specific set of dates in November 1944 that will make the Bad Love Gang the first humans to travel back in time and return safely."

Goondoggy immediately agreed. "You know me; I'm already in, because this sounds like a totally radical adventure!"

"That's my brother Goondoggy: always ready to rush into the jaws of death, not even knowing who, what, when, how, or why! Let's start with who; who are we going to try and rescue in 1944?" Willy asked.

Bowmar and I had created two stacks of files, and everyone was getting "homework" assignments to start reading about the nature of our proposed rescue mission. Bowmar passed out the files from the first stack to everyone as he took this question from Willy and ran with it: "Give me a show of hands, who has heard of the Holocaust?" Nearly all of the Bad Love Gang members raised their hands. Bowmar continued, "The Holocaust was mainly a Jewish genocide that took place during World War II between 1941 and 1945, when Nazi Germany systematically murdered six million Jews—which amounted to nearly two-thirds of the Jewish population of Europe. They also targeted and murdered some two hundred fifty to five hundred thousand Gypsies. In addition, Soviet citizens and POWs, communists, gay men, and Jehovah's Witnesses were routinely exterminated in the Holocaust. The Germans built six extermination camps in WWII occupied Poland: Auschwitz-Birkenau, Treblinka, Belzec, Chelmno, Sobibor, and Majdanek. BB and I are proposing a specific time-travel mission that will take the Bad Love Gang back to November 1944. At that time in history, only two of the Polish extermination camps were still operating: Auschwitz and Chelmno. We are planning a rescue mission to Chelmno, Poland, where it is estimated that three hundred forty thousand men, women, and children were killed by poisonous carbon monoxide gas, and then their bodies were burned. Chelmno is located in a rural area of east-central Poland and was winding down its

Holocaust killing operations in November 1944, to close permanently in January 1945. We know that we can only rescue a few Holocaust victims from extermination and certain death, given the method of rescue and extraction we are planning. We believe the lower profile characteristics and rural location of Chelmno will give us a strategic advantage to succeed there. Time travel is a tricky thing, and by saving lives we are potentially creating a 'wrinkle in time,' or altering history. We are proposing to you all tonight that saving even a single life from the Holocaust will make our time-travel mission worthwhile. This first 'homework' folder that I just handed to you has excellent review articles about the Holocaust and in particular, numerous details about Chelmno and that particular area of Poland in 1944."

Brianna "Cleopatra" Williams, Bowmar's sister, weighed in. "Bowmar, don't you be getting a bigger head than you already got—and God knows your head is too big already, with all those brain cells!" Everyone chuckled at that. "But I am proud of you and BB to want to make a little dent in some way in the Holocaust! What they did to all those people back then was horrific and unthinkable! We studied the Holocaust in school last year, and I have never understood why the Allies didn't try to do something more to stop it all sooner. I'm going on this mission, too. Baby, you can count me in!"

Aaron "Meatball" Eisen added to that sentiment. "As you all know, I'm Jewish; I come from a Jewish family and background. Listening to Bowmar talk about the Holocaust has given me goosebumps, butterflies, and emotions I can't describe right now. I don't know all the mission details yet, but you can definitely pencil me in for going to Chelmno to try and rescue people before they are exterminated."

Willy, trying to stay focused, spoke up again. "OK, we know who we aim to rescue, but how are we going to make that happen?"

I answered, "Despite your aversion to risk, Willy, this is a part of the mission that I doubt that even you can resist." I then passed out the files from the second stack to everyone.

Donny "The Runt" Legrande interrupted. "Oh, no. I have seen that glint in BB's eyes before! Brace yourselves, because the shit is about to start major league flying around here!"

"The Runt is right about one thing; there is going to be something about flying involved, but it's going to be big and silver, not small and brown!" I retorted.

"A Northern fairytale starts with 'Once upon a time,' but a Southern fairytale starts like 'Y'all ain't gonna believe this shit.' So get on with the small brown stuff, BB!" Tater exclaimed.

Everyone laughed, and I continued once they calmed down. "Late in the afternoon of November twenty-first, 1944, a brand new, U.S. Eighth Airforce B-17G Flying Fortress, on its third mission ever, landed in a grassy field in Kortenberg, Belgium adjacent to a Royal Air Force base, and sat in that field with its engines running. No one got off the plane. Twenty minutes went by; finally, a British officer went over to the plane and climbed on board. The plane was empty. It apparently landed by itself, after the crew had reportedly bailed out. The plane had been on a mission originating from East Anglia, England to bomb the highly-defended Leuna synthetic oil refinery near Merseburg, Germany. Supposedly, the plane got damaged by flak and was losing power and on its way down when the crew abandoned ship over Belgium. But the plane miraculously got its engines restarted after everyone bailed out, then landed intact by itself at a friendly Allied airbase. It got the nickname The Phantom Fortress, and the story has been very well documented in the annals of WWII. The complete story of the Phantom Fortress, along with everything you could want to know about the plane, its specifications and operations manual, is in your folder. We are going to be hijacking that specific plane, on that day, to run our mission."

Frankie "Spaghetti Head" Russo dove into the discussion, his Italian accent more pronounced in his excitement. "You know I'm Italian, right?" Everybody nodded. "I make it a point to never make the same mistake twice—I make it like, six or seven times, you know, just to be sure. So, BB, how's this all gonna go? You know we can't screw this up because we can't call the police or anything. Of course, in *my* home, we never call the police; we call family! I guess you can count me in, so I can help you not to screw this thing up!" Everyone had a good laugh at that.

"Bowmar and I have this mission pretty well planned," I reassured him. "We called you all together tonight so that we would have a three-month window to get all of our ducks in a row and be ready to launch our time travel mission on Monday, November eighteenth at one AM our time: so basically, really late on Sunday night for the first group."

Karen "Crisco" O'Sullivan had been listening carefully. She said, "First of all, by my count, everyone is greenlighting this time travel adventure, so I'm going. Hopefully it will get me out of some toddler-sitting duties at home, and I am certain that Cleopatra is going to need me for backup, with all you wolves baying in the moonlight in 1944. So BB, what did you mean when you said 'the first group?'"

I responded, "Good catch, Crisco! I have a special favor to ask of you in a minute. Let me give you all a better lay of the land here. The White Hole Project has a giant wardrobe room, so we will all be dressed to match our exact roles on the mission. We are going in two groups. On November eighteenth, we will launch Crazy Ike, Goondoggy, the Pud, and Meatball to a farmer's field in Chelmno, Poland. The four of them will arrive at seven AM local time. Crazy Ike speaks fluent German; he is going as a Nazi officer, and Goondoggy as his enlisted

Nazi helper. Meatball will be dressed as a Jewish peasant, and will be their prisoner. There is a church in Chelmno where the Holocaust victims are kept overnight before being transferred to be exterminated the next day. The plan is to get Meatball into the church with the rest of the prisoners, where he will try to gain their trust and then rescue them before they go to get gassed. The Pud's job will be to identify and mark a landing zone for the Flying Fortress, and find a country cottage for everyone to safely hide until we get there. They have three days to get that all done. On Tuesday, November twenty-first, we will land the hijacked Phantom Fortress to pick you all up, then fly to Belgium, where we will release the Holocaust folks we rescued. We will then make a short flight to land at Kortenberg, Belgium, just in time for all of us to be zapped back in time at four PM on November twenty-first—keeping the lore of the Phantom Fortress intact."

The Pud interrupted, "I hope that plane has VHF radio so you can let me know you're coming, BB. What if I don't find you a good landing zone?"

"The B-17 has fine VHF communication capability. And if we don't land to get you all, just remember: no matter what, at four PM on November twenty-first, you all are getting zapped back to 1974 Oak Ridge—regardless of where you are. All you have to do is stay alive, or as we Bad Love members say, 'Don't die!'"

I continued, "At twelve thirty AM here on Tuesday, November twenty-first, which will be five thirty AM in England, the second Bad Love group will launch in the time machine to the U.S. Eighth Airforce Base at East Anglia, England to hijack the 'Phantom B-17G Flying Fortress,' which carried the number designation five hundred forty-five, but had not yet been named. This was only its third mission ever, so it was virtually a new plane. Crisco, I want you to use your artistic abilities and design a large Bad Love emblem on a plastic appliqué that we can apply to the fuselage, and use it to name the plane Bad Love for this mission. We will fly the bombing mission with the flight group that day, but break away because of 'engine trouble.' We will then go to Poland to pick up group number one and the people they rescued. The folks going in the second group to hijack and fly the Bad Love plane are me, Willy, Tater, the Runt, Cleopatra, Crisco, Spaghetti Head, and Waldo. Waldo will be going as a two-star general, with special mission orders from the highest levels. We will be looking to temporarily 'borrow' it, or 'persuade' the plane's regular pilot and navigator to fly with us on this mission—and you all know how persuasive Waldo can be, when push comes to shove!" Waldo smiled and nodded his bald head in strong agreement, making us all chuckle.

"Finally, I have a wonderful surprise for all of you!"

Tater blurted out, "Yippee, Bubble Butt! You've already been more fun than a fart in a space capsule!" Everyone rolled on the floor with that one.

When the cackles died down, I went on. "Crisco, I will need you to be my nurse the day before or day of the mission. The way that the time machine tracks each of us to bring us back, no matter where we are in time, space, or location is by using a device called a global cosmic positioning device, or GCPD. These gizmos are about the size of a quarter, and have to be implanted in the cheek of your buttocks. The time machine locks on to that device to bring you back in time."

The Runt weighed in on that tidbit. "I'm a little worried about that thing going in my skinny little ass, but maybe Crisco could take a couple of them implanted in her big butt; we could just all hug her when it's time to be zapped!" Again, we all laughed so hard we cried.

I concluded, "One last thing, Bowmar is staying here with the white hole time machine to run the machine and controls, sending us all out for the mission and bringing us all back again. We have three months to study the mission parameters, decide what equipment, gear, and supplies to take, and rehearse together. We will be showing you the White Hole Project soon; it is like nothing you can imagine, so be ready to be amazed! Get your excuses lined up so that your families will know you will be away for a few days in November—or exactly thirty years, in the blink of an eye in this case! This will be an adventure above and beyond any movie or science fiction novel any of us have seen or read, only this is big, real, and 'bad!'"

CHAPTER NINE
READY FOR LAUNCH

"That's one small step for man,
One giant leap for mankind."
—Neil Armstrong

November 17th, 1974 at 10:00 PM local time,
The White Hole Project, Medical Bay, Oak Ridge, Tennessee

The entire Bad Love Gang had worked incredibly hard, long hours rehearsing as the two separate rescue groups and also as a team preparing for our coordinated time travel rescue mission, which would take place over the next four days. This was the day that we would launch Crazy Ike, Goondoggy, the Pud, and Meatball to a farmer's field in Chelmno, Poland to get the entire rescue mission sequence in motion. Everyone got their required mission clothing on the other side of the hall in the White Hole Wardrobe Warehouse, which had anything and everything to wear from across the globe during the WWII war years of 1942–1945. The four of them were already dressed to play their roles in Chelmno. Crazy Ike was posing as German SS lieutenant Eichenmuller, Goondoggy was his assistant, Meatball was their Jewish prisoner, and the Pud was a 1940's Polish commoner. Me, Bowmar and Crisco had decided to have a little fun on this night to get everyone to lighten up a bit. We decided to make the Medical

Bay into our pretend M*A*S*H unit, since we had a little important medical work to get done. All of us were big fans of the hit TV show M*A*S*H, which we had frequently watched together at Waldo's house during the '70s.

A Bad Love Gang line had formed outside the Medical Bay, as it was time for me and Crisco to implant the GPCDs into the butt cheeks of all the Bad Love Gang time travelers, including the eight of us who were leaving on November twenty-first. Bowmar was standing at the doorway of the Medical Bay dressed as a chaplain, playing the role of Father John Patrick Francis Mulcahy from M*A*S*H. Bowmar was acting the part of Father Mulcahy to the hilt, doing everything from baptizing to giving last rites as each person went in to get their respective GCPD surgically implanted. "Father Mulcahy" was letting everyone in line know that they had a choice to make. Most were thinking that meant they could opt out of the procedure, but the choice he gave to them went more like this:

"As you go through that door, you have a fantastic choice to make! You can choose to have the GCPD implanted in your right butt cheek...or you can choose to have the GCPD implanted in your *left* butt cheek. Just let Doctor BB Hawkeye Pierce know your preference, and have a wonderful life!"

Crazy Ike walked into the Medical Bay dressed as Nazi SS Lieutenant Eichenmuller. Bowmar/Father Mulcahy quipped, "I think you are long past blessing in *that* outfit, soldier—but all the same, good luck in there!"

Ike came through the door and Crisco, playing the role and dressed as Margaret "Hot Lips" Houlihan, gently took his hand and led him to the operating table, then told him to lay face down on the operating table and drop his pants so we could go to work. She introduced me as Doctor BB Hawkeye, and I was wearing army fatigues, a

Hawaiian shirt, and a lei. I purposely had my back turned to Ike as he walked in and lay down on the operating table. As I turned around, I had a hypodermic syringe and needle with Lidocaine in my right hand; in my left hand, I had a hacksaw. I asked Crazy Ike if he cared which hand I used first, and he nearly turned white. "You bastard, that's not funny!" he sputtered.

I replied, "Since you always tell us that you have 'buns of steel,' I figured I would need this hacksaw to get in there!"

Ike shot back, "Those are *abs* of steel, and who appointed you the doctor anyway?"

"The first rule of being a patient on the operating table is that you better be nice to the doctor who is about to operate on you. I plan on becoming a doctor someday, and I volunteer as a surgical orderly at the hospital where Crisco's mom works. That's as close to a real doctor as you're gonna get tonight, Buttercup! Hot Lips, give this Nazi a bullet to bite on and let's go to work!"

Crisco/Hot Lips and I proceeded to tease everyone as we methodically implanted all twelve GCPDs in the Bad Love Gang's right and left butt cheeks, their choice of sides. I implanted Crisco's GCPD and she implanted mine; it was the last one to get done. She joked that with my bubble butt, no one could ever tell it was there. I teased her that I closed my eyes while I put hers in, because I knew there was no way that I could miss the target with her massive buttocks! All the GPCDs came in boxes of two as matching pairs. Each person's matching GCPD was to be inserted in the white hole launch control panel in the process of sending that person out in time travel, a beacon for recalling that person at the specific designated time of return. After we had implanted each and every GCPD, Bowmar had numbered all the boxes and tagged the boxes with each person's name. We were extremely careful to make certain that each person's

GCPD box was kept separate from the others. The GCPDs would be our only connection to each person after they were sent back in time for our time travel rescue mission to November 1944.

November 18, 1974, 1:00 AM local time—The White Hole Project, Oak Ridge, Tennessee

The Pud, Meatball, Goondoggy, and Crazy Ike were all positioned on the soft central floor of the lower time machine racetrack with all their equipment and supplies, attached to them by the sturdy backpacks they were wearing. Their firearms were not loaded; the ammunition for those guns was packed in shielded containers that Bowmar had devised as an extra measure of safety. Their walkie-talkies and the Pud's VHF radio were also protected with extra shielding, since those things really needed to work flawlessly on the other end of their time travel today. Everyone was nervous except Goondoggy, who seemed comfortable "rushing into the jaws of death," as his brother Willy would teasingly say. We had all hugged, high-fived, and said, "See you soon on the other side!" so it was time for time travel launch. Bowmar ran the machine, and he would have to run it by himself to launch us—the second group—in three days. The rest of us—me, Waldo, Spaghetti Head, the Runt, Crisco, Cleopatra, Tater, and Willy—went to the second floor, where we could look down on the action and see better. We all stood and watched with anxious anticipation.

Bowmar proceeded to align and lock the upper racetrack of the time machine to the exact date of November 18, 1944, then engaged the lightspeed drive/cyclotron. Next, he docked the upper wide-mouthed opening of the telescopic exotic matter-lined funnel to the upper racetrack. Once that docking was complete and locked in place, he powered on the lower racetrack and all the other control panels.

The room lit up with active machinery, all running at capacity. He then connected the lower transparent end of the telescopic funnel to the lower racetrack. The four GCPDs matching the Pud, Meatball, Goondoggy, and Crazy Ike were precisely docked and locked in place in the mission control panel. Bowmar had already programmed in the global geographic coordinates for the farmer's field in Chelmno, Poland. The time travel machine was making a deep humming noise, combined with a higher whirr. The high-pitched whirring noise seemed to be emanating from the exotic matter-lined funnel connecting the two racetracks. The two noises seemed harmoniously linked.

There were two control buttons widely separated on the control panel: one marked *SEND* and the other marked *RECALL*. We could see the four of them sitting together in the eye of the lower racetrack. The clock struck 1:00 AM, and Bowmar hit the *SEND* button. At that very moment, Meatball, Goondoggy, Crazy Ike and the Pud vanished into thin air.

Even though that was exactly what we expected, we were dumbfounded and amazed anyway. Bowmar looked up at us and asked, "Do you all smell something odd?" None of us smelled anything up on the second floor, and within less than a minute, Bowmar said he couldn't smell it anymore. We didn't know whether to clap, cry, or both! Bowmar, who was certifiably brilliant, exclaimed, "That went exactly as planned; those four boys are sitting in a farmer's field in Chelmno, Poland at seven AM local time on November eighteenth, 1944! The eight of you are next, at twelve thirty AM our time on November twenty-first." His sense of confidence at that particular moment made all of us feel better.

November 21, 1974 at 12:30 AM local time, White Hole Project,
Oak Ridge, Tennessee

It was time for Bad Love Gang time travel rescue group number two to go back in time to the U.S. Eighth Air Force airfield in East Anglia, England, where we would "hijack" the new B-17G Flying Fortress #545 for our part of the mission. Waldo, Crisco, Tater, Spaghetti Head, Cleopatra, Willy, the Runt, and I, all appropriately dressed for our parts, collectively climbed into the "eye" of the lower racetrack with all our gear and supplies in our backpacks. We were a little nervous, but more excited to go and make this happen. We sat and watched as Bowmar went through the same general routine as three nights before. The clock struck 12:30 AM, and the last thing I saw was Bowmar's finger on the *SEND* button. The eight of us were gone in an instant, on our way to fly a plane that would soon carry the name Bad Love.

CHAPTER TEN

THE RESCUE AT CHELMNO, POLAND,
PHASE I: GETTING TO THE CHURCH

"The only thing we have to fear is fear itself."
—Franklin D. Roosevelt

Day One: Saturday, November 18th, 1944,

7:00 AM local time—Chelmno, Poland

Goondoggy, Crazy Ike, the Pud, and Meatball were zapped by the white hole time machine directly to Chelmno, Poland; they landed in a farmer's field just outside of town. The four of them shook their heads, looking at each other and their surroundings in amazement. They spent a moment taking in the crisp, early morning, fall air of November 1944 in the Polish countryside.

Meatball was the first to speak. "I don't know about you guys, but I have butterflies in my gut right now. I am Jewish and I know that this place has been an integral part of the Holocaust killings since the day Pearl Harbor was bombed by Japan, on December seventh, 1941. President Roosevelt said that day that would live in infamy—but he did not know that in addition to the Japanese bombing of Pearl Harbor, the Holocaust started here in Chelmno, Poland at precisely the same time."

Meatball was correct about the historical significance of the Chelmno extermination camp. It was the first place where Jews were gassed in the WWII genocide known as the Holocaust, which took the lives of six million Jews and 250,000–500,000 European Gypsies. On the evening of December 7, 1941, the "Final Solution," or Holocaust, began when about 700 Jews from the Polish village of Kolo arrived at Chelmno. On the following day, all of them were killed at a local manor house (called "the Castle") in the village of Chelmno, using carbon monoxide poisoning in gas vans specially designed as carbon monoxide killing machines. The dead victims were then taken in those vans to a clearing in the Rzuchowski Forest near Chelmno, where they were buried in large common graves. Later, in the spring of 1942, two crematoria were built to burn the dead bodies of the Chelmno victims. It is estimated that 330,000 Holocaust victims were killed at Chelmno from December 1941 through April 1943. The Chelmno extermination camp was temporarily closed in April of 1943, and reopened in the late spring of 1944.

The Holocaust activities at Chelmno in 1944 differed from what had occurred during 1941–1943. The victims were brought from Kolo, Poland by a local branch railway line directly to Chelmno during the day, and were taken to the village church to stay that night. The next day, after spending the night at the church, they were taken directly to the Rzuchowski Forest by truck. In the forest, two wooden huts had been constructed: One of them was designated as a place to undress, because the victims were told they were going by van to a bath house. The other hut was a clothing and baggage storage and processing site. After getting undressed, the unknowing Holocaust victims were directed into the back of gas vans and killed with carbon monoxide gas as before. They were then driven about 500 feet to crematoria (furnaces), where the corpses were burnt. It is estimated that another 10,000 Holocaust victims were killed using this methodology at Chelmno in 1944.

The Pud, Goondoggy, and Crazy Ike calmly reassured Meatball that they had all made this time travel trip to Chelmno on this specific day and time in history to make a small but real difference for some of Chelmno Holocaust victims. Part of their mission agenda for that day was to find Chelmno's rail connection station coming from Kolo, Poland. Most incoming Jewish and/or Gypsy victims would be arriving by that route, and would be taken from the train station to the village church to stay for the night. It wouldn't be as large a number of people as it had been during 1941–1943, when an estimated 1,000 victims were murdered every day. In 1944, "only" 10,000 total victims were murdered all year. By November of 1944, the Chelmno operation was really slowing down, with just one of two crematoria remaining operational in the Rzuchowski woods. That furnace and the remaining Chelmno operation were totally destroyed in January 1945.

The four of them gathering themselves and their gear to go to work were an unusual sight. Crazy Ike was dressed as a Nazi SS officer, Goondoggy was a German SS enlisted soldier, and the Pud could pass as a common Polish citizen. Meatball appeared to be a Jewish peasant and their prisoner. He had a yellow Star of David patch sewn onto the back of his shirt at the right shoulder, and a brown flat cap on his head. Their overall plan for day one was to scout out the road leading from Chelmno to the Rzuchowski Forest, and find the exact spot where the wooden huts and one remaining furnace were located. They would find a good ambush point along that road, where they would stop and steal the truck carrying the Jewish/Gypsy prisoners— and Meatball, who would also be on board when the time came. After identifying the ambush point, they planned to go into Chelmno to find the village church and spy on the Jewish and/or Gypsy arrivals to the church from the train station or elsewhere.

Crazy Ike spoke excellent, fluent German due to his childhood upbringing. The story line was that he was posing as a Nazi SS officer from Lodz, Poland; Goondoggy was mute but he was a good German SS soldier, accompanying Crazy Ike. Once they determined that the day's Holocaust victims had been taken to the church to spend the night, they would then take Meatball as their Jewish prisoner to the church and leave him there. Meatball would spend the night with victims and get to know them, gaining their trust; he would be getting on the truck with them in the morning to go to the Rzuchowski Forest extermination camp. Failure was not an option for this rescue operation, or Meatball could die in the Holocaust.

In the meantime, the Pud had two objectives: One was to explore the local countryside and the lay of the land, to find a potential landing zone for the B-17. The second objective was to find a suitable hideout for the four of them and the Holocaust folks that they rescued, where they would need to stay until Tuesday morning. If all went as planned, a brand-new B-17G Flying Fortress named Bad Love would land on Tuesday at about high noon to scoop them all up, then fly them to freedom and safety in Belgium. The Pud was hoping to accomplish at least one of his two objectives on day one. The four of them had maps of the area and excellent long-range walkie-talkies to communicate their progress. They all group hugged, then Goondoggy said, "Don't get lost, Pud; we need a place to stay!"

"You look like shit in that Nazi uniform. You'll have to find something else to wear, if you want to stay in the house that I find!" he replied.

Crazy Ike chimed in. "So, Pud, you and what army are gonna stop us? Grow some balls and go find a runway for that big ass plane to land on Tuesday!" And with that typical Bad Love banter, they parted ways.

They had been zapped back in time and space to a farmer's field due north of the village of Chelmno, east of the narrow-gauge railroad that connected Kolo, Poland to Chelmno. Meatball, Crazy Ike, and Goondoggy headed west toward the railroad tracks. The Pud headed east toward the small village of Ladorudż, Poland, where he hoped to find an empty country summer cottage somewhere along the way—and a long enough, flat enough field for the B-17 landing zone. They had come prepared, and their local maps were well researched and superb.

Meatball, Crazy Ike, and Goondoggy did not have to go far to get to the road. The narrow-gauge railroad tracks that connected Chelmno to Kolo ran generally parallel to the road. They stuck close to the tracks, staying out of sight from the road, and walked northwest roughly halfway to the Rzuchowski Forest killing camp, which was only about 2.5 miles from the village of Chelmno. It was here that they discovered the perfect place for their planned ambush. A small road intersected with the main road to the forest camp, and ran behind the camp; they could take the truck unnoticed past and around the forest camp to get to the hideout, which the Pud was busy finding. Goondoggy and Crazy Ike would steal two motorcycles in Chelmno before sunrise and lay in wait at this intersection to ambush the truck carrying Meatball and the Jewish/Gypsy prisoners. The Pud and Meatball would drive the truck to the Pud's countryside cottage hideout location. Crazy Ike and Goondoggy would give the truck a motorcycle escort in their German Nazi uniform attire.

The plan was coming together. The three of them high-fived and then turned to walk southeast, parallel to the tracks, to the village of Chelmno. This perfect route would end at the train station in

Chelmno, which was close to the Church of the Nativity of the Virgin Mary, where the Jews/Gypsies who were unknowingly destined for death by carbon monoxide gas poisoning were held overnight prior to their transfer to the Rzuchowski Forest extermination camp the following morning. The walk to the village, going unnoticed by anyone, took a little less than an hour.

In the meantime, the Pud was making some progress. He had headed east and approached the small village of Ladorudż, Poland. He crossed a road that on the other side had long, flat, fairly wide plowed fields that extended back in a northeasterly direction, and ended at the edge of a pine tree forest. There was forest on both sides and at the end of the fields. Since it was November, there was no one working or tending to the fields this time of year, and it was a sparsely populated area. He made a note on his map of this location, then paced down the fields to the edge of the forest pine trees. He estimated 4,000–4,500 feet (give or take) from the road to the edge of the forest. Interestingly, as he got to the forest's edge, there was a dirt road leading through the forest; he saw another dirt road in the forest to the east. He made the simple decision to take the dirt road in front of him and see where it led. He was hoping it would lead to a nice summer cottage, abandoned for the winter. It wasn't quite that simple, but he was on the right track.

The Pud radioed Goondoggy, who had left his walkie-talkie turned on for communications. Goondoggy was looking through his binoculars at Chelmno village when he heard the Pud's signal. He grabbed the walkie-talkie and asked, "Hey, Pud, you having any luck out there?"

The Pud replied, "That's a big ten-four, Goondoggy! I found a suitable landing zone adjacent to the small village of Ladorudż and now I am following a dirt road through the forest looking for a place for us to stay. Tell Crazy Ike that we're gonna use that Nazi officer uniform he's wearing as our door mat!"

Crazy Ike, who was sitting in the grass next to Goondoggy, smiled. He grabbed the walkie-talkie and said, "Listen, Pud, you little shit, you better start lifting some weights and working out, because I'm gonna make *you* our door mat when I get there!"

"I found a big-ass, black dog who hates Nazis. He's already hungry, and I am not gonna feed him a thing for now. When he sees you, I'm cutting him loose. Rub a little German chocolate cake on your crotch to give him a scent to follow!" With that reply, the Pud signed off.

At the same time as the Pud's update via walkie-talkie, the Saturday train from Kolo, Poland to Chelmno was on its way. It was all of a forty-minute train ride and on this particular Saturday, there were only thirteen souls on board who were destined for the Chelmno extermination camp the next day. The Chelmno killing operation in November 1944 was officially closed, but the Rzuchowski Forest work crew were still there "working" until January 17, 1945, when the German SS soldiers shot everyone (two Jews escaped that night) and burned everything to the ground. These thirteen unfortunate souls (eleven Jews and two Gypsies) riding on the train were among the last to suffer in the Holocaust at Chelmno, Poland in its waning days of operations. All of them had been told that they were going to go to work for the German war effort in the east, and that they would be fairly treated and receive good food. There were only two guards watching over them and making certain to get them to the Chelmno church, where they would spend the night under separate guard.

Among the thirteen prisoners on board the train were the entire Roth family of five, which included Daniel and Mazel Roth; their two daughters, twelve-year-old Zelda and ten-year-old Rhoda; along with Mazel's mother, Rachel Soros. The five of them lived together in the small village of Wrzaca Wielka, and had nearly gone unnoticed during the Holocaust era; Daniel had quietly run the family farm and maintained a low profile. The night before, the local German police and German SS soldiers had essentially surrounded their small village and surprised them during their Sabbath (Shabbat) celebration. Before Friday nights' Sabbath dinners, it was customary to light candles and sing two songs: one to greet two Shabbat angels into the house, and the other praising the women of the house for all the work they had done over the past week. Daniel had four hard-working women in his household; he was deeply proud of his family. As they were singing the second song together, German SS soldiers suddenly banged so hard on the front door with their rifle butts that it seemed like the door would bust off its hinges. The SS soldiers loudly yelled, "Open the door *now!*"

There was no time to prepare or react. Daniel told everyone to be calm, and not put up a fight. Mazel and Rachel locked arms and held their two terrified daughters closely. Daniel was much more afraid of harm coming to his family of four cherished women than he was for himself. He resolved to be cooperative in the hope that they could all stay together, no matter what else happened. Daniel opened the door and two heavily armed SS soldiers quickly entered. They told the family to pack one suitcase for all of them, and that they were being taken away in the morning to work for and support the German war effort. The Roths were given ten minutes to pack that single suitcase and Daniel instructed Mazel to comply. Ten minutes later, the Roth family was escorted out the door, loaded into the back of a covered truck with a guard, and driven to a jail in Kolo for the night, which they spent in a holding cell. The German soldiers and local police reassured Daniel that the family would be kept together—so long as they did exactly as they were told every step of the way. Any misstep or problem would result in their separation.

Sitting directly in front of the Roths was an elderly couple, Asher and Avigail Goldberg, and a young boy named Ben. Sitting behind the Roth family was a Roma (Gypsy) mother named Vadoma Loveridge and her five-year-old son, Barsali. Vadoma's husband (and Barsali's father) Manfri had been shot to death by a German SS soldier in a scuffle that had occurred when the Loveridge family was being transported by train to the Lodz, Poland Ghetto just over a year before, in late 1943. In the confusion and rush of soldiers to the scene, Vadoma was holding on to Barsali (who was age four at that time) tightly; an elderly man grabbed her arm from behind and barked, "Come with me, now!" They managed to slip away in the mass confusion, and the elderly man led Vadoma and Barsali to his house in Lodz, not too far from the Ghetto. That elderly Jewish man and his wife, Asher and Avigail Goldberg, then housed and safely kept Vadoma and Barsali in their home in secrecy for an entire year, hoping for the war to end.

This was not an uncommon occurrence in Poland during World War II. Polish Jews were among the principal victims of the German-organized Final Solution, or Holocaust. During the entire wartime German occupation of Poland, many devoted Polish Jews and Polish citizens risked their lives—and the lives of their families—to rescue Jews and Gypsies from the Germans. The Polish people rescued the most Jews during the Holocaust, more than the citizens of any other country.

Two days prior, on Thursday, November 16, 1944, Asher Goldberg brought home an eight-year-old Jewish orphan boy named Benzion (Ben) Kaplan. The boy was on the run from authorities after his adoptive parents were detained; he had escaped on foot. Asher witnessed this event, saw where the child was hiding, and decided to help. Asher's heart was larger than his luck on this particular day; some German/Nazi sympathizer saw Asher take the child into his house and called the police. The police raided the Goldbergs' home on Thursday evening and took all five of them into custody. On Friday, two of the Lodz police officers were making a trip to Kolo and decided to take the five of them along by truck to be "processed" at Chelmno over the weekend. Vadoma, Barsali, Asher, Avigail, and Ben all landed in the same holding cell in Kolo as the Roth family on Friday night. The ten of them were put on the train to Chelmno together on Saturday.

In the same train car headed to Chelmno was the Lieb family: David, his wife Sarah, and their eighteen-year-old daughter, Hannah. The Lieb family was from Klodawa, Poland, which is only ten miles northeast of Kolo. In 1941, more than 1,500 Kłodawan Jews were killed by the Nazis at the Chelmno extermination camp. During the wartime occupation by Nazi Germany, their town was renamed Tonningen. The town was responsible for the largest operating salt mine in Poland, extracting rock salt along with salts of magnesium and potassium. David and his family were initially spared deportation because his heritage was hidden from the Nazis. He was felt to be indispensable, as the lead construction engineer who knew everything about the ongoing maintenance and operation of the Tonningen salt mine. Unfortunately, one of the young, brazen Nazi guards had flirted too much with David's beautiful daughter Hannah, and she was feeling threatened. A few days before, that guard's life had ended under a large, heavy pile of rock salt that had mysteriously fallen from a conveyor belt that failed to stop properly. David was a prime suspect in the accident, and the decision was made to send the Lieb family to "help with supporting the Nazi war effort in the East." The three of them were driven to Kolo on Saturday morning to be taken by train from there to Chelmno for processing.

There were a total of thirteen prisoners of different backgrounds all brought together by fate this day on the train to Chelmno. Their common fate was not to be forced to work for the German war effort in the east as they had been told. They were scheduled to be extermi-nated the following day by poisonous carbon monoxide gas, and their corpses would then be cremated—all because of their race and heritage. The clock of fate was ticking, but because of time travel and Bad Love, their destiny was changing.

After signing off with the Pud, Goondoggy turned his gaze and binoculars the opposite direction and saw the train from Kolo in the distance, coming their way. He had Meatball double check, and Meat-ball confirmed that he could see the train approaching. Crazy Ike sat up straight and said, "It's time to take our Jewish prisoner into town, and meet the train as it pulls into the station. We can join whatever prisoners that they bring from Kolo today, and go with them to the church for holding tonight. Given my rank of SS lieutenant, none of these shitheads are going to mess with me!"

"Just don't let me die as your Jewish prisoner, or this shithead will be seriously messing with you from beyond the grave!" Meatball replied.

Crazy Ike smiled and said, "It's gonna be OK, Meatball. Play the part and get to know your fellow prisoners tonight so they are ready when we rescue all of you tomorrow morning."

Crazy Ike, Goondoggy, and their Jewish prisoner Aaron Eisen (AKA Meatball) then proceeded to walk straight into town, following the course of the tracks directly to the small railroad station. No one was in a hurry to speak with them because Crazy Ike was dressed as a German SS officer and outranked the local police. Plus, it was Satur-day, and other than the incoming train, the village was quiet from a military perspective. Five minutes after the three of them walked into the train station, the train from Kolo arrived. Other than a few local civilians who departed from the train first, there were no passengers other than the two local police guards who came off the train with eleven Jewish and two Gypsy prisoners. Crazy Ike walked right up to the lead guard and in perfect and authoritative German, he said, "I am Lieutenant Eichenmuller, and we have a Jewish detainee to be processed through here tomorrow. We would like to accompany you and your prisoners to the church."

The guard answered with the German version of yes sir: "Jawohl, Lieutenant."

Meatball stood between Crazy Ike and Goondoggy as the thirteen prisoners were being directed off the train by the two local police guards. The Lieb family was the last to get off the train with David first, Hannah second, and Sarah last. The second guard in the rear had grown impatient with the slowness of their departure, and decided to push Sarah in the back using his rifle butt. Sarah nearly fell face first as she was pushed off the train; Hannah, sensing the problem, turned just in time and caught her mother.

David instinctively turned, then confronted and shoved the rear guard who had used his rifle butt on Sarah's back. As the guard began to raise his rifle to point the barrel directly at David's chest, Meatball bolted in front of David to protect him. At that instant in time, Meatball's eyes met Hannah's for the first time. His eyes were like those of a lovable golden retriever, and her eyes were as deep as Venus; both felt an unmistakable attraction in the midst of terror. The guard had put his finger on the trigger, and at that moment, Crazy Ike stepped up. He forcefully said to the guard, "If you pull that trigger, you will join these prisoners and be processed right along with them tomorrow! Lower your weapon, soldier, now!" The guard demurred and complied as ordered, apologizing to Lieutenant Eichenmuller (Crazy Ike) for his temper.

The entire group then collectively headed for the Church of the Nativity of the Virgin Mary. It was a ten-minute walk to the church, where the fourteen prisoners (including Meatball) were led inside, then told to "make themselves at home for the evening." The church was a safe place for the night, and the group felt a sense of relief from the events of the past few days.

CHAPTER ELEVEN
THE RESCUE AT CHELMNO, POLAND,
PHASE II: GETTING TO THE COTTAGE

"There are only two ways to live your life.
One is as though nothing is a miracle.
The other is as though everything is a miracle."
—Albert Einstein

After the door of the church was shut, there was a continuous guard duty posted until the fourteen people inside were taken to the Chelmno extermination camp in the Rzuchowski Forest for processing early the next morning. The guards knew that if anyone escaped, they would be held accountable and taken for processing themselves. Crazy Ike and Goondoggy watched as Meatball went into the church with the rest of the prisoners and the doors were shut behind them. Crazy Ike thanked the guards, and asked what time the group would be transferred in the morning. One of the guards replied that the transfer truck always came early, at about 7:00 AM as a rule—so they could get their work done early, and "enjoy the rest of their day." Goondoggy felt like vomiting after that comment, and looked a little sick. The guard asked, "What is wrong with him?"

Crazy Ike replied, "He has been a mute since a botched surgery when he was a child, but he is a good soldier and does exactly as he is told." With that, Ike and Goondoggy departed and proceeded to check out the rest of the village.

Crazy Ike and Goondoggy walked through the village, keeping to themselves during their reconnaissance on foot. They were hoping to find two motorcycles that they could come back and steal very early Sunday morning. They made their way to and spied on the village police station, where they spotted four parked motorcycles. There was a single BMW R75 and three BMW R35s, all parked together.

The German military was big on motorcycles during World War II and kept BMW in a high production mode. The BMW R75 was produced from 1941–1946 as a World War II German motorcycle and sidecar combination. The very tough R75, with its crankshaft-driven sidecar, proved itself to be a major asset to the German army. Its specifications included a 745cc air-cooled, four-stroke, overhead valve, twin-cylinder engine producing 26 hp. It could get 52 miles to the U.S. gallon, with a range of 225 miles, and had a top speed of 60 miles per hour. The R35 was also a popular military motorcycle, but had no sidecar; a single cylinder 350cc engine provided 14 horsepower, and this bike also had a top speed of about 60 miles per hour. The R35 frame was made from massive-looking pressed steel sections, and it was a sturdy, reliable bike that could navigate through woods and rough terrain. Crazy Ike wanted in the worst way to steal the BMW R75, but the potential need to ride through the woods made stealing two of the R35s a better choice. Trying to make any detours through the woods on a motorcycle with a sidecar didn't make much sense. He and Goondoggy determined to come back before sunrise on Sunday morning and make off with two of the R35s.

Meanwhile, the Pud was making more progress. The winding, dirt country road that led away from the landing zone he'd found, dead-ended at a paved road. The terrain had become hilly and was fairly heavily forested there. He turned left on the paved road listened intently and watched carefully for any traffic; he did not want to be seen. The scenic road was lined with pine trees and hardwoods that had dropped most of their leaves for the fall. He passed a few driveways where he could see cottages farther back in the woods. With lights burning and chimneys spewing smoke, he knew someone was home. He walked for a few hours on this road and eventually came to a driveway with a cottage barely visible in the woods, but with no sign of life or recent activity. He quickly investigated, and it appeared to be closed for the winter. He systematically checked the front and back doors, then moved on to the windows. Luckily, a bedroom window was unlocked and he made his way inside. The furniture was covered with sheets, and there were no dirty dishes in the sink or other signs of recent occupancy; the place was so clean it might have been closed up that day. There were two bedrooms and an open space containing the main room and kitchen, and a single bathroom. It was quaint and cozy, by 1940's standards! The biggest stroke of luck was a bicycle parked in the main room that would come in handy almost immediately.

It was 3:30 PM, with about 90 minutes of daylight left when the Pud pinged Goondoggy on the walkie-talkie. Goondoggy and Crazy Ike were walking back to the intersection where they planned to accomplish the ambush in the morning. The chosen location was roughly halfway to the Rzuchowski Forest killing camp, making it slightly less than a 1.5-mile walk from the village of Chelmno. Goondoggy answered the Pud's ping with a question.

"Hey Pud, did you find us a castle in the woods?"

The Pud answered, "Oh, yes! It is the spitting image of the castle at Disneyland, and you can hear Jiminy Cricket from Pinocchio singing 'When You Wish Upon a Star,' playing in every corner throughout the castle. Mickey and Minnie are serving me afternoon tea as we speak, and there is a tall dog named Goofy with a southern drawl like Tater, who wants to sit in your lap when you get here."

"You and Goofy go hand-in-hand, buddy; you might have just found your own replacement!" Goondoggy teased.

"Let me ponder that," the Pud responded, "but yes, I found a cottage. Fortunately there is a bicycle here, because I walked a long way today to find this place. I need to get out of here and meet you guys before the sun sets." Goondoggy gave him directions from where they all had parted ways that morning, and they signed off. The Pud made haste and good use of the bicycle, hurrying to reunite with Goondoggy and Crazy Ike by sunset. The three of them would camp near the ambush site that night.

In the church, the prisoners were getting acquainted with each other—especially Meatball and Hannah. Hannah had recently turned eighteen years old; Meatball was only sixteen, but surprisingly mature for his age. He introduced himself to the Lieb family as Aaron Eisen, and quickly added, "Everybody calls me Meatball."

David Lieb shook Aaron's hand and said, "That was an incredibly brave thing for you to do, stepping in between me and that soldier's gun pointed at me today, Meatball. What possessed you to do that?"

"My dad died when I was eleven years old. He was my hero, and meant everything to both me and my mom," Meatball replied, his eyes welling up with tears. "I guess in that instant, I didn't want your daughter or wife to experience what me and my Mom experienced in losing my dad."

Hannah's heart melted more than ever, and a bolt of emotional lightning shot through her spirit from head to toe. She felt a little lightheaded; without thinking, she tightly hugged Meatball, kissed him on the cheek, and thanked him from the bottom of her heart. For his part, despite how scary and tough this day had been, Meatball suddenly felt like it was the best day of his life.

Avigail Goldberg, her husband Asher, and the eight-year-old orphan boy, Benzion (whom Asher had rescued two days prior), were sitting in earshot of the Liebs' and Meatball's conversation. Avigail was 75 years old and Asher was 77, but they were both in great shape and physically a bit younger than their actual chronological ages. Avigail was super spunky for her age, and not shy with her observations. She could see that Meatball and Hannah were attracted to each other and said to the two of them, "How about I distract the guard out there with my exotic charm and beauty, and the two of you slip by and go on a date tonight?"

David Lieb protested, "Don't you think that they would need my permission?"

Avigail retorted, "I should suppose that stepping in front of that gun pointed at you today should suffice!"

David smiled and conceded, "Yes, I think he earned my trust today!"

Vadoma Loveridge walked over to all of them holding her son's hand. She introduced herself and Barsali, then asked Meatball where he was from, since he was not on the train with the thirteen of them. Vadoma was an attractive woman in her mid-thirties with beautiful, jet-black hair, a feminine voice, a mysterious accent, and piercing eyes. She seemed to project a sense of maturity and discernment. Rather than immediately answer her, Meatball took this as an opportunity to call the entire group together, and asked the Roth family to gather around with the rest of them. Once they were all gathered together, they introduced themselves to the group one by one until last but not least, it was Meatball's turn.

Meatball wasn't sure how this would go, but decided to tell the truth as much as possible. "What I have to tell you is totally true, but

I will accept and understand if you cannot believe it all. First, you must know that all of you have been taken from your homes and lives because you are Jewish or Gypsy. You are being persecuted because of your heritage, beliefs, and race. By the time this War is over, the Nazis will have exterminated or murdered six million Jews and two hundred fifty to five hundred thousand Gypsies in what will one day be called the Holocaust. The fourteen of us are not being 'processed' for transport to work for the German war effort tomorrow; we are being 'processed' for extermination by poisonous gas, and then cremated afterward."

Everyone gasped and Avigail blurted out, "I *knew* those Nazi bastards and their sympathizers have been lying to our faces! All the rumors we have been hearing about the fate of our people being shipped away from the Lodz Ghetto are true!"

Rachel Soros, Mazel Roth's mother, enquired, "How do you know all of this, Meatball? You still seem quite young, and you speak with authority—as though you know this for certain."

Meatball continued, "I am here from another place and time, specifically to help rescue the thirteen of you. You will know that I am telling you the truth because early tomorrow morning, a truck will come to take us to be processed. During our truck ride to the Rzuchowski Forest, we will be rescued from certain death by the two men who brought me to the train station today."

Daniel spoke up and asked, "Why would the Nazi lieutenant and the other soldier with him help you to rescue us?"

"Because they are both with me, and they are not Nazis. We are all Americans, here on a secret mission to rescue you. After tomorrow morning, we will all be hiding together until Tuesday at noon. An American B-17 Flying Fortress named Bad Love will be landing nearby to pick us up at about noon on Tuesday and taking all of you to Belgium, where you will be safe and set free."

Vadoma then asked, "What do you mean by another time and place?"

"Somehow, I was afraid someone would ask that question, and I don't expect you to believe this. Me and my team, or gang, of friends traveled here from a place called Oak Ridge, Tennessee, in the United States, in the year 1974 using a time travel machine called the White Hole Project. We cannot stop the Holocaust, but we can and will save the thirteen of you."

"Wow, I can't wait to see that plane!" Ben Kaplan exclaimed.

Vadoma looked Meatball in the eye and said, "I actually believe you, Meatball."

For the rest of the night, the fateful thirteen people (plus Meatball) who were spending the night in the church together bonded with each other; they told their life stories, and traded their opinions regarding the validity of Meatball's claims. Given all that they had witnessed during the German occupation of Poland since 1939, there was no doubt among them about what Meatball had called the Holocaust. Most of them did not know what to make of Meatball's claim to be from the future, but they could tell that Meatball was genuine and cared about all of them and their welfare. It was a bona fide case of love at first sight for Hannah and Meatball. Every moment that Meatball was not answering other peoples' questions, he and Hannah were talking about anything and everything.

Day Two: Sunday, November 19, 1944 at 4:30 AM local time

Crazy Ike and Goondoggy had discreetly made their way back to the Chelmno village police station. It was quiet and still dark outside as they approached the parked motorcycles. Someone had taken one of the BMW R35s since they were there late the previous afternoon. Three motorcycles remained, two R35s and the R75 with the sidecar. Crazy Ike whispered to Goondoggy, "I want that R Seventy-five!"

Goondoggy whispered back, "I wish I had a new Corvette convertible and a beautiful blonde riding next to me, but if wishes were horses there'd be more shit on the streets! Let's get those two R Thirty-fives and get the hell out of here!"

They made quick work of it and quietly pushed the two bikes away from the station. Both Crazy Ike and Goondoggy had grown up riding dirt bikes and various motorcycles, and they were both excited to give the R35s a try. When they had pushed the two motorcycles far enough down the road to be well beyond earshot of the village, they started the bikes and rode back to the intersection where they had camped for the night and planned the ambush.

The Pud was relieved to see them back as planned with the two motorcycles. He had been outlining the route back to the cottage on the map. The route would bypass the Rzuchowski Forest extermination camp. Then they would turn east, go across the road to Kolo, and continue southeaster through the villages of Przybyłów and Ladorudzek on their way to the country cottage that he had found, which was a few miles from the landing zone. Fortunately, they would be traveling very early on Sunday morning, and given their uniforms and vehicles, they did not anticipate any major obstacles. This area was not a major military base in November of 1944; it was designed as a site to exterminate Jews and Roma (Gypsies), and to go largely unnoticed by the world around it. No one really expected or anticipated a rescue operation to save and liberate Jews and Gypsies.

They reviewed their plans for the ambush, assuming that it would happen shortly after 7:00 AM local time. The Pud would take his bicycle a little more than a mile down the road, then radio Crazy Ike and Goondoggy when the truck came by. Goondoggy was to be lying under his motorcycle on the road at the intersection, as if he had been in an accident, with Crazy Ike tending to him. With Crazy Ike dressed as a Nazi SS Lieutenant, the truck would stop to render help. Crazy Ike would then turn his pistol on the driver and guard. Goondoggy and Meatball would duct tape both of them while Ike held them at gunpoint, and they would take them as prisoners. They would ultimately leave their two prisoners at the landing zone, figuring that there would be a lot of people investigating that site after they flew out of there on Tuesday at noon. Meatball could drive the truck holding the thirteen rescued souls and two new prisoners while the Pud navigated. Crazy Ike and Goondoggy would escort the truck on their motorcycles. Once at the cottage, they would hide the vehicles in the back until they all left on Tuesday to meet the plane.

At 6:45 AM on Sunday morning, the truck transporting the group at the church to be processed at the Chelmno extermination camp pulled up to the front door. The night shift guard at the door—Aleksander Piontek, age nineteen—was assigned to ride in the back of the truck with the prisoners. There were always at least two guards per truck (one in the front and one in the back) to make certain no one escaped during the drive to the forest for processing. The driver that morning, Jakub Nowak, was fairly new and young for the job at age seventeen. The drive to the Rzuchowski Forest, where the fourteen prisoners would be made to undress in a wooden hut and then directed into the back of a gas van and killed with carbon monoxide, was less than three miles away.

Aleksander opened the front door and told the fourteen people inside the church that it was time to get into the truck and leave. They all filed into the back of the truck, and as Avigail passed Aleksander, she looked at him and said, "You should be ashamed of yourself, young man!" Aleksander didn't understand why she decided to speak, but ignored her as best he could, even though her words stuck in his mind for a while. Aleksander got in the back of the truck and yelled at Jakub to move it.

Jakub, the driver, headed away from the church and out of the village of Chelmno toward the extermination camp in the Rzuchowski Forest. At 7:00 AM on Sunday morning, the town was completely quiet. In the back of the truck, Meatball was sitting next to Hannah. Even though he was confident in his friends Crazy Ike, Goondoggy, and the Pud, his heart was beginning to race as adrenalin flowed through his system. Running the ambush plan through his head, he grabbed Hannah's hand and held it tight. Hannah knew from their talk the night before that things were about to change.

In the front of the truck, Jakub Nowak was taking it slow and easy, trying to enjoy the cool, partly sunny, Sunday morning drive. On the other side of the road, he saw a Polish teenager riding a bike toward town. *How early for that guy to be out on his bike this Sunday morning*, he thought. As the truck went by, the Pud stopped and radioed Goondoggy that the truck was headed their way, and it was time to execute the plan. The Pud then circled around on his bicycle and headed back after the truck.

In the ambush intersection, Goondoggy got down on the road and positioned his black BMW R35 motorcycle on top of his legs, turning himself face down. Crazy Ike had his R35 parked upright and knelt beside Goondoggy, pretending to be giving him aid. Crazy Ike, in classic Bad Love fashion, said in a baby talk voice, "Aw, Goondoggy, are you feeling a wittle sick this morning? Do you have a temperature? Can I get your mommy? Do you need your Teddy-weddy bear and blankie?"

Goondoggy replied, "You're gonna need *your* mommy, big time, in about two seconds, you piece of shit!" They both smiled and laughed, then Ike could see the truck coming. Goondoggy said, "You better have that German Luger pistol ready to go, Ike!"

"It's fully loaded with one in the chamber. Here we go!" With that exchange, the truck pulled up and stopped.

Jakub saw what he perceived to be a motorcycle accident and recognized that a German SS officer was kneeling down on the pavement giving assistance to a German soldier underneath his motorcycle. He brought the truck to a stop and turned off the engine. Aleksander yelled, "What's going on up there?" Jakub replied that there was a motorcycle wreck, and an SS officer was assisting in the street. Aleksander then yelled, "We better give them some help!" He jumped out of the back of the truck and came around to the front as Jakub got out. The two of them walked up to Crazy Ike, AKA, SS Lieutenant Eichenmuller, side by side. As they approached, Meatball told everyone in the back of the truck to stay there and wait. Meatball got out and peeked around the side to watch the plan unfold. He also saw the Pud down the road in the distance, riding his bicycle their way.

When Jakub and Aleksander got to Crazy Ike, Jakub was to his left and Alexander was on the right. Ike needed a better vantage point to pull his pistol. He ordered the two of them to lift the R35 up and away from Goondoggy, who was still face down on the pavement. Jakub and Aleksander did as they were ordered to do. As the two of them lifted the BMW R35 up and away, Goondoggy suddenly sprung to his feet. Aleksander and Jakub looked up to see that both Crazy Ike and Goondoggy pointing their German Luger pistols at their chests. Aleksander asked, "What's this all about?"

Crazy Ike replied, "This is what is known in America as a stick up! We are stealing your truck and prisoners, and taking your sorry asses with us. Make a move and I'm blowing your heads right off your shoulders. Got it?"

They both said, "Yes, we got it." Goondoggy had pulled out 2 rolls of duct tape and Meatball was now on the scene. They proceeded to quickly duct tape their prisoners' wrists, then bound their arms behind their backs, and also taped their mouths shut. As they walked Jakub and Aleksander to the back of the truck, the Pud arrived on his bicycle, looked at Jakub, and said, "Yep, that was me you passed back there, butthead." The Pud put his bike in the back of the truck and said, "Hi, I'm the Pud; glad to meet all of you!"

Avigail looked at the rest of the group and blurted out, "Don't you like these guys? They must get this way from watching those Western cowboy movies in America!"

Meatball picked up Aleksander's rifle, then ordered him and Jakub into the back of the truck. Making them sit back to back, he duct taped their torsos together first, then taped their legs together; they weren't going anywhere or saying anything to anyone. Meatball handed the rifle to David and asked him if he would mind guarding the prisoners. David winked at Meatball and responded, "Can I shoot them if they move too much?" Aleksander's and Jakub's eyes got big and white and wide.

Meatball winked back at David and said, "You can shoot them whenever you please!"

Daniel chimed in, "I can help with that!" Hannah was smiling at Meatball the whole time, knowing that he was truly her knight in shining armor.

Meatball got in the driver's seat of the truck and the Pud climbed in on the passenger side. He told Meatball, "You're taking a left on this crossroad, following it down and then around to the right, to circle behind the forest." Crazy Ike and Goondoggy were on their bikes and ready to go. It was only about 7:20 AM; the whole ambush had taken less than ten minutes.

They got moving and headed to the country cottage, using the route that the Pud had outlined on their maps. The work crew at the Rzuchowski Forest extermination camp was not on a particular schedule on Sunday mornings, and did not call the guard office in Chelmno until 10:30 AM to enquire if anyone was coming today. This created a bit of general confusion for the socialist government office, trying to figure out if something had gone wrong while putting the pieces of a puzzle together. In other words, the right hand did not exactly know what the left hand was doing.

At about 4:00 PM on Sunday afternoon, enough people had talked and traded notes to determine that two motorcycles were missing from the police station, along with a truck, two guards, and fourteen prisoners who did not make it to the forest camp for processing. Calls were placed to the Kolo station, but no one was in a hurry for fear that anyone who seemed to be responsible for this failure might have to take the blame, and end up dead at the hands of the Nazis in charge. Those involved decided to wait until morning and start fresh, hoping that the problem would fix itself.

The drive to the country cottage took longer than expected because it was a slow and circuitous route to get there on the backroads. They made it there unnoticed, and parked the vehicles behind the cottage, well out of sight from the road. The upside was that they had a place to stay: a roof over their heads in a secluded area, with back access to the B-17 landing zone. The downside was that there were nineteen of them—thirteen rescued Holocaust victims, four Bad Love rescuers, and two local police guards whom they had taken prisoner. All nineteen of them, staying in a quaint two-bedroom, single bathroom country cottage, until mid-morning on Tuesday.

CHAPTER TWELVE

THE RESCUE AT CHELMNO, POLAND, PHASE III: GETTING TO THE PLANE

"I'm not afraid to die,
I just don't want to be there when it happens."
—Woody Allen

By the time the truck and two motorcycles were hidden and thoroughly camouflaged with tree branches behind the cottage, and the group went inside talking about the rescue and events of the last 24 hours, it was time for a midday meal. Everyone was absolutely starved. During this time when everyone else was preoccupied, Meatball had lit the wood burning stove and got busy looking through the kitchen cupboards and a small, narrow food pantry in the corner. He found some jarred foods including borscht (beet soup), sauerkraut, dill pickles, smoked sausage, wholemeal (whole wheat) flour, cooking oil, baking soda, vinegar, and salt. He combined the wholemeal flour with water, a splash of vinegar, a few dashes of salt, a little baking soda, and some cooking oil; despite having no eggs, he was on his way to making fresh bread. In the midst of this activity, Hannah and Vadoma noticed him at work in the kitchen. They were simultaneously amazed and intrigued to see this young man taking the initiative to start cooking for everyone.

Vadoma came up behind Meatball, looking over his shoulder. She asked, "What is a young man doing in the kitchen? We should be the ones cooking the meal now. Is this what it means to be from the future? I'm going to start calling you future boy every time I see you doing something I can't explain!"

Simultaneously, Hannah was standing pressed snugly to his right side. She asked if she could be of help, batting her eyelids and saying, "May I help you knead the dough, Meatball?" She managed to get her hands in the bowl with his, and the sparks were flying again!

Watching this encounter, Goondoggy rather loudly said, "You all might as well know now, Meatball is the designated cook for all our wild adventures and camping trips. He knows how to cook up something when the pickings are slim to none. That guy can make a tasty meatball out of sawdust, roots, and molasses! And that my friends, is how he came to be known as Meatball by the Bad Love gang!"

The entire group ate together, starting with the borscht and followed by Meatball's fresh bread with the smoked sausage, sauerkraut, dill pickles, and some assorted nuts that were also bottled up in the pantry. While Sarah Lieb and Mazel Roth both ate, they also kindly fed the two prisoners (Aleksander and Jakub) as everyone else was eating. The two prisoners remained bound while they were fed, but they did get to witness the continued bonding of the group as a whole. There is something about breaking bread together that brings people closer, and to this starving group, this ranked as one of their best ever meals. They all shared stories of the past, hopes for the future and laughter. Daniel and Mazal's two daughters, Zelda and Rhoda, both gave Meatball, Crazy Ike, Goondoggy, and the Pud all big hugs and told them this was the most fun they'd had in a while. Vadoma's son Barsali and the orphan boy Benzion had found a deck of cards, and were playing together trying to stack cards to build card houses. It was an afternoon filled with the best human emotion: relief!

The afternoon went by quickly, and the sun set early on that Sunday in November. Everyone figured out who was sleeping where in the cramped but cozy country cottage. Before going to sleep, the Bad Love boys gathered around to plan for the next day. The Pud would lead the group to the landing zone that he had identified. Crazy Ike and Goondoggy would take the two motorcycles and check out the roads all around the landing zone; that way, they could plan to be at the best vantage points to watch for Nazi soldiers or local police, then give fair warning to the rest of the group to hide, fight, or run. Once the B-17 Flying Fortress named Bad Love was on its approach, they knew for certain that all bets were off. The landing would make a huge, unmistakable scene for this area of rural Poland.

While Crazy Ike and Goondoggy were on their reconnaissance mission, Meatball and the Pud would be making certain that the landing zone was free enough of holes and ruts for the big tires of the B-17 to land and take off again safely. In addition, they would gather the thin ends of tree branches that would mark the centerline of the landing zone on Tuesday, creating a line of sight for the incoming plane. They would collect and pile those branches in the woods on Monday, for placement on Tuesday. Finally, the Pud was supposed to build a smoky fire at the end of the landing zone on Tuesday at 11:00 AM so Bubble Butt could see the smoke and orient the B-17's landing approach that way as well. They would get that ready to go tomorrow as well; now it was time to get some rest.

Day Three: Monday, November 20, 1944 at 7:30 AM local time

Mazel Roth and her mother, Rachel Soros, conspired to make breakfast, along with Vadoma and Avigail Goldberg—perhaps improving on Meatball's bread recipe a bit. There were a few jars of jam and some honey in the pantry, and it was enough to get everyone going. Hannah was up early, and Meatball had shared their plans for the day with her. She and her family had visited friends in this area before; it was not far from Klodawa, where she grew up. She offered (insisted) to help today because she was familiar with the area—and mostly, I suspect, because she wanted to spend the day with Meatball.

She had preemptively asked for her father David's permission; he was now very comfortable with Meatball and the rest of the Bad Love gang. Meatball brought it up with Goondoggy, Crazy Ike and the Pud. Crazy Ike said, "So long as she doesn't slow us down, I don't care." Hannah heard him. She walked right up to him and put her right foot on top of Ike's left foot and said, "I don't mean to step on your feet or anything, Crazy Ike, but I'm a year older than you, and grew up helping my father in the Klodawa Salt Mine—which is not exactly a gentle place. I can take care of myself, and you too, if you get yourself in trouble!" Goondoggy and the Pud started laughing, and Meatball beamed with pride.

"OK, let's go scout out that landing zone!" Meatball said.

The Pud had given Crazy Ike and Goondoggy the directions to the dirt road turnoff a few miles down the road to the right, which then dead ended at the back of the landing zone. Meatball asked them to carefully check and make sure that the dirt road was passable using the truck with the thirteen rescued folks in back for the ride to the landing zone Tuesday morning. They all had their walkie-talkies to stay in communication with each other. Goondoggy and Crazy Ike took their motorcycles and headed on their way. They also planned to check the proposed landing site when they got there, and had a lot of ground to cover today to get the lay of the land for the next day's planned evacuation.

The Pud, Meatball, and Hannah set out on foot with tools in their backpacks for cutting small branches, and army shovels to fill any ruts or holes along the planned path of the B-17 landing zone. Not too far from their cottage, Hannah recognized a path leading off the road. She said, "I am sure that I have been down that path before; it leads to a grove with a fishing pond. I recognize it because of that giant pine tree growing in the middle of that path. It is a beautiful area in there!"

"We'll have to spend a day there sometime and catch some fish!" Meatball joked.

She smiled sweetly and responded, "I'll make sure of that, Meatball."

They kept walking and came to the dirt road turnoff just as Goondoggy and Crazy Ike appeared on their motorcycles. Goondoggy spoke up. "I have good news and bad news. The good news is that Pud, you did good with finding this landing zone. From the back end of the landing zone where this dirt road dead ends, to the country road where the field starts, is over four thousand feet. It is generally flat, provided you make a few small repairs. For the centerline of the landing, look from where this dirt road dead ends to the old farmhouse, just across the country road at the other end of the field. Make the centerline connect those two points. Ike and I rode that line several times, and it is smooth enough for the big wheels of the B-17. It should have no major issues landing, with its two big wheels straddled along that line." Crazy Ike also mentioned that the dirt road was easily passable—so long as they drove slowly, because of the ruts and turns—using the truck in the morning to get the rescued folks to the landing zone.

The Pud asked, "So what's the bad news?"

Goondoggy replied, "We are discovering lots of country roads on either side of the forest surrounding the landing zone. Once the Germans and local police see the plane coming in for a landing, this place is going to get real hot, real fast; we better make our escape as fast as greased lightning!"

Meatball commented, "You know Bubble Butt, AKA 'Mr. Plan for Everything Bad;' he'll have something up his sleeve when this place heats up! You should probably start feeling sorry for anyone who gets in our way!" They agreed to meet back in a few hours, then Goondoggy and Ike took a right turn. The pair headed further down the road they had come in on, which was parallel to the other side of the forest lining the edge of the landing zone.

The Pud, Meatball, and Hannah walked the winding dirt road until it dead-ended at the landing zone. Along the way, Hannah asked, "Who is this 'Bubble Butt' guy, anyway?"

"You can call him BB for short, but he is the guy who basically masterminded this entire scheme to rescue you guys from your fate at the Chelmno extermination camp," Meatball answered.

The Pud chimed in, saying, "Yeah, he has somehow managed to plan all of our adventures growing up, since we were little kids. For some reason, he has total confidence in getting things done; he tries to make it a little bit dangerous, and a whole lot fun. Our Bad Love Gang motto is 'Live dangerously, have fun, don't die!' Speaking for myself, I feel the most alive whenever we go on these crazy adventures. I sure never thought that I'd be a time traveler, and right here on this day!"

The three of them came to the end of the dirt road and found themselves staring straight down the field to the old farmhouse that Goondoggy had mentioned. They could see some of the tire tracks from Goondoggy's and Crazy Ike's motorcycles going directly in that line of sight. To their left, in the back corner of the landing zone,

Goondoggy and Ike had left a small "present." They had gathered four large logs to make a square fire pit and had stacked dried sticks beside it, ready for a smoky signal fire, with dry leaves as the starter fuel. That was one item off their to-do list.

The Pud, Meatball, and Hannah proceeded to walk the imaginary centerline of the landing zone from the back to the front. There was forest on either side of length of the field, but it was open at the other end to the country road. Hannah walked the centerline with the Pud thirty feet to her left and Meatball thirty feet to her right. The wingspan of the B-17 was nearly 104 feet. They decided to try and make certain that there were no hidden holes or other obstacles, and brought the army shovels to make the landing strip as smooth as possible. They wanted a flat landing path 100 feet wide, as much as they could make that practically happen, and the field itself was at least 600 feet wide all along its length. The B-17's landing wheels were 56 inches in diameter with 16-ply tires, and could take small bumps or ruts in stride. Fortunately, using the centerline connecting the back of the landing zone to the old farmhouse, the strip of field they walked and groomed was generally flat with no deep ditches or ravines on close inspection. They walked down to the country road and back, filling small holes and leveling small rises. It was tedious work that took several hours, but they talked and joked as they went. The Pud filled Hannah's ears with many stories about Meatball, some of which were true and others that somewhat stretched the truth, and the time flew by. In the end, they felt proud and satisfied with the product of their work: a landing strip over 4,000 feet long and 100 feet wide.

As they returned to the dirt road that ended at the landing zone, they saw Goondoggy and Crazy Ike were back. The Pud thanked them for getting the signal fire ready to light. Goondoggy, who loved playing with matches when he was too young to be trusted (and had accidently set a section of woods on fire in Oak Ridge), quipped, "Why would I let you plan a fire when I'm so good at it?"

The Pud responded, "You definitely have superior credentials in that department, Goondoggy!" The five of them then agreed to cut and gather small tree branches into a pile at the back edge of the landing zone, which they would use to mark the centerline of the landing zone in the morning. They were a bit worried about doing that task too early, just in case someone came by and saw a long, straight, suspicious line of fresh small branches in the field. Goondoggy and Ike parked their motorcycles, and they went different directions to gather the branches from the forest—with Meatball and Hannah staying together, of course.

While they all piled up small branches, Hannah and Meatball "somehow" wandered out of sight. Hannah was standing on a large, irregular stone trying to tear a low branch from a pine tree and started to lose her footing. Meatball saw her slipping, and managed to perfectly catch her as she came off the stone. He was looking into her eyes, but wasn't quite ready for what happened next. Hannah pulled his head toward hers and summarily locked her lips with his. At first, Meatball was a bit shocked that she had initiated the kiss, but that thought quickly melted into oblivion. It was like magic, and he couldn't even begin to grasp what he was feeling and experiencing. Their lips were a custom fit together, a match made in heaven. Hannah was also on cloud nine, and at age eighteen, knew what she was doing. She loved Meatball and was busy expressing that love in the heat of the moment. Suddenly, as if awoken from a dream, they both heard the Pud yelling for them, and the magical kiss was over.

The Pud couldn't see them, but he did yell in the correct direction. He indicated that it was time to go, and that Goondoggy and Crazy Ike were going to finish while the three of them started their walk back to the cottage. It was by this time mid-afternoon, and a somewhat cloudy November day had given way to beautiful sunshine with partly cloudy skies. While the temperature had been in the low 40s (Fahrenheit) when they left that morning, it had reached a "balmy" 61 degrees (which was warm for that part of Poland in November). Meatball, Hannah, and the Pud started down the winding dirt road, heading back to the paved road that led to the cottage. Meatball was holding hands with Hannah, and trying his best to sort out feelings that he could not quite grasp, at age sixteen. All he knew was that he was love struck, and there was some kind of electricity being conducted back and forth between his hand and Hannah's.

Hannah was likewise feeling very warm and cozy, happily fuzzy in spirit. She had talked to various friends about what love felt like. However, their answers generally seemed a bit superficial. And in a short time frame, their relationships had always given way to boredom and endless routines. Hannah had never before been in love, but this guy Aaron, or Meatball—who claimed to be from the future—had exactly what she admired in her own vision of the perfect partner. He was confident in himself, but humble about it. He was strong but gentle, and a good listener. He could laugh at himself (or at his friends), and he could definitely be spontaneous and go with the flow of things. Finally, his bravery in the face of a German rifle pointed at his chest yesterday had sealed the deal. Hannah was in love, and she was sure of herself.

The three of them had taken a left on the paved road and were nearing the cottage. Crazy Ike and Goondoggy pulled up on their motorcycles, and informed them that everything was ready for the airborne evacuation, except for laying down the branches to mark the centerline for the plane to land. Crazy Ike saw Meatball holding hands with Hannah and remarked, "If I had a beautiful girl like her, Meatball, I wouldn't be headed straight back to the cottage." He gave Meatball a big, overdone wink and a cheesy grin.

Hannah, who had again spotted the path to the fishing pond on her left, looked at Crazy Ike and said, "For once, Ike, you actually said something that makes a little sense. I think Meatball and I will take a nice walk down to the fishing pond before we head back to the cottage." At this point, Ike was starting to feel a bit jealous; why couldn't he have found a love interest on the trip? As they parted ways, Hannah told them to tell her dad that she and Meatball would be home by dark.

Hannah and Meatball headed down the small path to the meadow and fishing pond that Hannah had remembered from her youth. The path was lined with mostly pine trees, and it opened into a grassy meadow with an idyllic fishing pond that reflected the autumn sun as it sank lower on the western horizon. They saw a few wrinkles on the smooth surface of the water where some fish were surfacing for their food. They found a place in the grass by the pond to spread their coats on the ground, and sat down next to each other. Meatball settled on Hannah's left side, with his right arm around her shoulders.

"This place is beautiful, Hannah, and I feel like I could spend the rest of my time on earth right here with you. I'm having feelings that I never imagined could be real or possible, but I know they are real!"

Hannah turned into his arms, looked into his puppy dog eyes and said, "Meatball, I feel the same way—and I just have to say, I love you like crazy!" As he started to reply, about to say "I love you too, Hannah," she did it again: She started it! Meatball realized that Hannah had started to unbutton his shirt and unbutton her own, going back and forth from top to bottom. They embraced and locked lips again, only this time there were no further interruptions, just stars and fireworks exploding for the next 45 minutes. When they were done, they lay on their backs with Hannah's head on Meatball's shoulder. The world and all its troubles were gone, as if nonexistent. They were at total peace with each other, and neither of them would ever, ever forget it.

The sun was setting and just below the horizon when they headed back to the cottage. They managed to time it perfectly, walking in as it was getting dark outside. Dinner was being served, and everyone was sharing their stories of the day. David and Sarah Lieb were glad to see Hannah; both hugged her as she came inside. Crazy Ike winked again at Meatball, but Meatball wasn't biting and ignored Ike's warped mind. Dinner was amazing for a second night, and everyone was exhausted and ready to get some rest afterward. It was truly amazing that this group had bonded so well, but perhaps that is what sheer survival during a World War does: It breaks down any and all barriers, and makes you grateful just to be alive, safe, and with people who care. Tomorrow was another day and the concept of safety would be left at the cottage.

The Bad Love boys gathered around again at bedtime to review the plans for the airborne evacuation the next morning. Crazy Ike, Goondoggy, and the Pud (the Pud would ride on the back of Goondoggy's motorcycle) would all leave first by motorcycle, and the three of them would get the small tree branches placed along the landing zone's centerline. Afterwards, Goondoggy and Ike would take their motorcycles to their vantage points on either side of forest that lined the landing zone to keep watch as the plan progressed. They both had rifles with scopes as well as Smith and Wesson 9mm pistols, along with plenty of clips and extra ammunition. The Pud would build the smoky signal fire at about 11:00 AM, just in case the Bad Love B-17 came early. In addition, the Pud would have his VHF radio on, waiting to hear from BB as the B-17 approached. Meatball would bring all thirteen of the rescued folks to the landing zone at about 11:15 AM using the stolen truck, trying to time it as the plane was making its approach to land. All of them would have their walkie-talkies to communicate as needed. They all knew full well that this was going to be dicey, and they had to make the evacuation go like clockwork. They also had quiet confidence that BB would somehow show up and make this happen. When they finished talking it through, their hearts were beating faster as they thought about what they were planning to do.

Day Four: Tuesday, November 21, 1944 at 7:00 AM local time

Everyone was up early, and it had been a restless night's sleep for almost everyone. A virtually brand new Eighth Air Force B-17G Flying Fortress named Bad Love, on its third mission ever, hijacked and commandeered by the rest of the Bad Love Gang, was about to bomb a Nazi German oil refinery, then come to pick them all up near Chelmno, Poland, and take the Holocaust victims to safety in Belgium. How crazy was that!? Yet it was happening; it was time to finish what they had started.

They ate their final breakfast at the cottage and everyone (except the two prisoners, Aleksander and Jakub) chipped in to clean the cottage like no one had been there. Meatball asked Hannah to write and leave a thank-you note for the cottage owners. When she finished, he signed it *Bad Love* and left a 1933 gold eagle on top of the note. The gold eagle was a United States $10 gold coin issued by the United States Mint from 1792 to 1933. It was the least they could do, he thought, for using the cottage the past few days.

At 7:20 AM Goondoggy, Crazy Ike, and the Pud took off on the two motorcycles. Turning right and heading down the paved road, they passed a man walking his dog. He couldn't help but stare at the three of them, and this raised a red flag in Goondoggy's mind. A little further down the road, he pulled over and had the Pud radio Meatball to warn him to lay low for a while and keep a lookout.

Most of the morning went as planned. Crazy Ike, Goondoggy, and the Pud went first to the landing zone. They took the branches that they had piled up the day before and laid them in a straight line, visually connecting the dirt road opening at the back of the landing zone to the front door of the old farmhouse, but stopping at the country road at the other end of the field. As they did so, they actually complimented the Pud for how flat he, Meatball and Hannah had made the landing strip. After marking the centerline for the B-17 landing—which took nearly two and half hours—Goondoggy and Ike took off on their motorcycles to their vantage points, reminding the Pud to keep his walkie-talkie close by. For his part, the Pud went to the back of the landing zone and made sure that he had enough extra wood and dried leaves to keep a smoky fire burning. He lit the fire at 10:45 AM, turned on his VHF radio, and began to intermittently transmit: "Bad Love One, this is the Pud. Do you read me?"

At precisely the same time, Meatball was getting the thirteen rescued folks into the stolen truck for the ride to the back of the landing zone. He had David Lieb and Daniel Roth help get their two prisoners (Aleksander Piontek and Jakub Nowak) into the back of the truck, as well; their arms and hands were duct taped behind their backs, but their legs were free to use. They had been well cared for as prisoners, and both of them knew that this group meant them no real harm. Nevertheless, Meatball instructed David and Daniel to keep a close watch on them, and to take them out of the truck in back of the landing zone when they got there. They would tape their torsos together again, preventing the guards from raising an alarm while sitting there. They would not be going anywhere until rescued by their own police force, after all the dust settled from the plane leaving.

As everyone got in the truck, Hannah told Meatball that she was riding up front with him. He smiled at her and asked, "Do I have a choice?"

She smiled back and responded, "Of course not!"

"OK, 'Sergeant Hannah,' I'm 'Lieutenant Meatball,' and I am ordering you to get in the truck now!" She felt a little tingle go down her spine, and got in on the passenger side.

Everybody was on board and at 10:55 AM they left the cottage, turned right on the paved road, and headed to the landing zone. Unknown to them at this moment, and not much more than 10 minutes behind Meatball, was a German truck driven by Nazi SS sergeant Karl Becker, accompanied by privates Werner Koch and Manfred Weber. Becker, Koch and Weber had been following a lead called in that morning that some strangers had been staying in a summer cottage in the country-side near Chelmno, reported by a neighbor who was out walking his dog. They were hoping to find the truck and Jewish prisoners that had been hijacked on Sunday, November 19th. They managed to arrive at the cottage at about 11:10 AM, minutes after Meatball had departed. The nosey, Nazi-sympathizing neighbor showed up and pointed them in the direction Meatball was headed. Becker, Koch, and Weber were in pursuit of the stolen truck and its occupants.

At 11:10 AM, Meatball had already made the right turn off the paved road, and was driving on the winding dirt road leading to the back of the landing zone. The Pud radioed on the walkie-talkie to check in, and Meatball reassured him that he would be there in just a few minutes. The Pud then returned his attention to his VHF radio and continued intermittently transmitting, "Bad Love One, this is the Pud, do you read me? Bad Love One, this is the Pud. Do you read me?" At 11:17 AM, the radio finally barked back at him.

"Yes, we read you, Pud; loud and clear. This is Bubble Butt—over!" From that moment on, time became blurred as the airborne rescue mission rapidly unfolded. Prior to this moment, Bubble Butt and the rest of the Bad Love Gang had one heck of a crazy, adventurous Tuesday morning on the inbound B-17G Flying Fortress that had originated in East Anglia, England, and currently bore the name Bad Love.

CHAPTER THIRTEEN

THE B-17G FLYING FORTRESS NAMED BAD LOVE

"You don't win a war dying for your country.
You win a war by making some poor bastard die for his country."
—George S. Patton

November 21, 1944 at 5:30 AM local time, England

We were zapped by the time machine directly to the East Anglia Airfield in eastern England, and landed in the deep grass adjacent to one of the runways among neat rows of parked B-17G Flying Fortresses. We were all on the grass in the same orientation to each other as we had been on the time machine stage at the time of launch. Two of us had been "stung" by lightening in the midst of the time tunnel transfer process. I was stung on the right flank, and had an interesting and distinct jagged lightning-bolt scar forming already. The Runt was stung in the middle of his left hip, and he didn't care to pull his pants down for us to all check it out!

The global cosmic positioning device (GCPD) technology had obviously worked, and the return clock was ticking. We were all physically sitting together on a U.S. Eighth Air Force Airbase in East Anglia, England at 5:30 AM on November 21, 1944; we had until 4:00 PM local time in Belgium to execute our rescue plan.

According to our research, we were looking for the B-17G aircraft numbered 545. Fortunately, our B-17G was so brand new that it hadn't been officially named or painted; this was only the third mission for this plane, after arriving at the East Anglia airbase from the Boeing Company on the U.S. mainland. We were looking for the shiny, new plane #545 with no name. As I mused for a moment about the plane with no name, my "music brain" started playing the song **"A Horse with No Name,"** by America.

I quickly recovered by pinching myself, then slapped myself on the right cheek and focused on our new reality: this airfield in eastern England in 1944. There were rows and rows of B-17G bombers, all ready to roll forward onto feeder runways that led to the takeoff airstrips. It was time to go to work!

The eight of us split up into two groups to find our plane among the rows of B-17s and communicated with our walkie-talkies. Just as the sun was barely coming above the eastern horizon, my group found plane #545 and called the others to come to our location. With the sunrise just beginning to reflect on the aluminum fuselage of plane #545, the eight of us stood together facing the plane, mesmerized by the awesome beauty and majestic power of this brand-new Boeing B17-G bomber sitting proudly in front of us, ready to fly, fight, and rescue! We were going to take this big bird from England and fly over Germany to bomb a synthetic oil refinery, then continue to Poland, rescue Holocaust victims, and then take them on to Belgium to finish our time travel mission. I was covered in goosebumps from head to toe, and my heart was nearly exploding!

The B-17 Flying Fortress was legendary, one of the most revered WWII allied warplanes. B-17s participated in almost all U.S. theaters of operation in WWII, including North Africa, the Middle

East, Europe, and the Pacific. However, the B-17 was most effective in the Allied bombing campaign against Nazi Germany's industrial complex, including ball bearing factories, airplane manufacturing, and oil production. The B-17 went through many modifications during WWII, indicated by the capital lettering after the number 17. The plane directly in front of us that we were all profusely admiring was the definitive G model, which had entered wartime service in September of 1943. The B-17G model had a maximum speed of 287 MPH; a range of 2,000 miles; a service ceiling of 35,800 feet; four Wright Cyclone 9-cylinder, air-cooled, radial engines producing 1,200 horse power each (4,800 total horsepower); and this beast of an airplane was all-in defended with *thirteen* 50-caliber machine guns. The plane was overbuilt to withstand a great amount of physical punishment and keep flying. Known as a pilot's pleasure to fly, the B-17G carried a 4,000-8,000 pound bomb load depending on the mission parameters. Earlier models were more vulnerable to a frontal attack from German fighter planes, but the B-17G came with an added remote-control Bendix "chin" turret, fitted with twin 50-caliber machine guns to fight off any frontal attacks.

The B-17G model was loved and admired by the wartime press corps as well; it frequently made for majestic pictures of allied airpower in newspaper headlines. Probably the most celebrated and widely recognized aircraft of World War II, it was a typical practice for the B-17 crews to cleverly name their planes and paint their creative design and associated name on the nose of the aircraft—many times using sexually suggestive themes. In the 1940s, this practice sometimes came across as vulgarity to the public at large, being long before Elvis Presley's gyrating pelvis, rock and roll, miniskirts, and Woodstock.

Going with the flow of the times, I had instructed our artistic Crisco to prepare our Bad Love emblem on a clear, adhesive-backed plastic sheet and bring it with us for this moment. I shuffled over to Crisco and put my arm around her shoulders. Together, we faced this new B-17G, and I said, "It's time to make this plane the badass queen of the skies that she is meant to be. Go ahead and get some help from the crew, and get our name up on that starboard nose; and in addition, Crisco, keep your fat in the can!"

Crisco replied softly in my ear, "Anything you say, Colonel 'Full-of-Shit'. I mean, Bubble Butt."

Next, I instructed the Runt to go to work with his planned magic for juicing the fuel mixture and engines to give our four Wright Cyclone 9-cylinder radial engines an extra boost of power for this mission. The Runt had been researching this mandate for some time, but had remained rather secretive about what he had been calling his

"B-17 white lightening." He seemed confident that we would get up to an extra 5–10% horsepower boost, bringing our total to nearly 5,300 horsepower—if it worked. We would need that extra edge to shorten our takeoff run in Nazi-controlled Poland.

There was one more special modification that needed to be implemented for our mission today. I had asked each member of the Bad Love crew to give me the name of their favorite road song, or favorite song in general. Willy was our resident audiophile and sound expert; I had met with him privately weeks before our mission to discuss bringing our B-17G sound and intercom system up to 1974 standards. Willy discreetly came up with a plan to use the latest Koss headphones for our intercom system. In 1974, Koss engineers developed a second phase in headphone or "stereophone" listening. The Koss Phase 2 was the world's first headphone to feature panoramic source controls. The addition of a phase switch and panoramic source dial allowed the listener to manipulate the soundscape, making it sound as though they were standing shoulder to shoulder with the musical performers themselves. Willy made it so our communication with each other during the flight, and the music that I chose from the cockpit, would play beautifully in everyone's ears. I gave Willy the green light to get all the crew stations and crew wired for sound, as per his plan.

Our cherished and appropriately christened Bad Love B-17G had been fully fueled and loaded with ammunition and bombs before we arrived. The sun was coming up, which meant that the plane's actual captain and crew would be arriving soon for their preflight checklist and departure. I instructed everyone to get in the plane, take their assigned positions, and wait for Waldo and me to deal with the captain and crew when they came. Shortly thereafter, at about 6:10 AM local time, we saw several crews beginning to arrive by jeeps and trucks and walking to their respective B-17s. Whether by fate, luck, or destiny, the

KEVIN L. SCHEWE, MD, FACRO

captain of our plane pulled up in an army jeep with only his navigator, no crew with them—yet.

I looked at Waldo and said, "It's time to stand and deliver, Waldo! Let's see if our grand plan will sink or swim."

"Listen here, Bubble Butt; if it starts to sink in any way, my Smith and Wesson is gonna throw it a lifeline real quick!" Waldo sounded just like John Wayne at that moment. It made me relax, and smile just a bit.

CHAPTER FOURTEEN

BAD LOVE TAKES TO THE SKIES

"There are many ways of going forward,
but only one way of standing still."
—Franklin D. Roosevelt

W aldo, 43 at the time, was dressed as a U.S. Air Force two-star major general; I was dressed as an Air Force colonel, trying my best to look older than just one month shy of age sixteen. We walked up to meet the B-17 pilot and his navigator as their jeep came to a stop in front of our plane. The men got out of their jeep and appropriately saluted both Waldo and me. The pilot introduced himself as Air Force Captain Jack Smith. The navigator introduced himself as Sergeant Darby Nelson, and mentioned that he was also qualified as a bombardier. Waldo introduced himself as General Paul Thompson, and I introduced myself as Colonel Kevin Schafer. Waldo started the conversation by handing Jack a copy of our "official" orders, apparently signed by General Dwight Eisenhower and Secretary of War Henry L. Stimson. Waldo stated, in a commanding and authoritative voice, "Jack, we are here for a top-secret, classified mission. We need both you and Sergeant Nelson to fly with our crew, already on board; we do not have a need for the rest of your crew today." Jack carefully read the orders, which essentially gave us carte blanche to do as we wished, and instructed the recipients to cooperate in any way possible with our needs. He looked at me and Waldo with a bit of amazement and said, "May I have a word with the two of you in private, while Sergeant Nelson stays here with the jeep?" I became apprehensive about this request, but Waldo was as cool as a cucumber.

Waldo calmly said, "Sure, Jack; let's take a short walk together."

Waldo, Jack, and I then headed around toward the tail of Bad Love, while Darby took a seat in the jeep. I noticed that Waldo had discreetly unbuttoned his pistol holster as we started to walk. Once we got well behind Bad Love and out of hearing distance from Darby, Jack looked at us and said, "What took you bastards so long? I have been waiting a full week for you and a crew to get here without knowing any details of our plans, other than we were going to take plane number five forty-five on a secret mission. Was there a problem with the white hole time machine?" Waldo and I were stunned beyond belief by this development.

Being so intimately involved with the operations of the time machine, I was the first to speak. "So Jack, what year did you launch in the time machine from Oak Ridge?"

Jack replied, "I launched on March fourteenth, 1945, with a target date to land here in East Anglia, England on November fourteenth, 1944. I am an experienced pilot trained for special operations, chosen as the first person to launch in the White Hole Project. I was told that I would either be brought back in one day, or a crew would join me in three days with further instructions for our top-secret, classified mission. By secret protocol, I was only told just as much as I needed to know each step of the way."

I was beginning to put this puzzle together, and already developing concerns about the potential implications. Waldo seemed relieved that I was taking the lead at this point, re-buttoning his pistol holster. I continued with my line of questioning. "Jack, did you have any issues traveling through the white hole tunnel coming back here in time?"

Jack replied, "Well, as a matter of fact... While I was in the white hole, I saw a bright flash of light—just like a lightning bolt—and simultaneously felt like I got stung in the ass by a rattlesnake!"

"What side of your ass?"

"What the hell does that matter, Kevin?"

I said, "It matters a lot, Jack. Before you launched, they implanted a small, shiny, metal sphere in your right or left butt cheek." Jack and I connected at that moment.

"Oh, shit. I forgot about that damn thing; I got stung on the same butt cheek as that device was put in!"

My mental puzzle came together. I said, "Brace yourself, Jack; I have some unsettling news for you. But once I let you know the truth, we have a mission to fly and you are our pilot."

"OK, give it to me straight, Kev."

"Jack, we all launched here this morning from this very day thirty years in the future: November twenty-first, 1974. For your reference, I was born on December seventeenth, 1958. Your GCPD was damaged in the white hole tunnel, on what was probably the inaugural time travel test launch—and you have been stuck in time! They probably tried to bring you back, but with your GCPD knocked out, the first test was a failure; having lost you in time, they may have cancelled the mission or stopped the entire project. That might at least partially explain why the White Hole Project seemed abandoned when we found it, in 1974. I know this sounds impossible and bizarre, but you are going to have to trust me; I will be able to explain more to you as we go. I do have some good news for you."

Jack, looking a bit pale and puzzled asked, "What could be the good news?"

"I have an extra GCPD with me. Bowmar and I were worried about the GCPDs being a proverbial weak link in the chain of our mission, so we brought extras."

"Who the hell is Bowmar?" Jack asked.

"Don't worry about him; worry about me implanting another GCPD in your ass today, and how that's gonna feel!"

The three of us started walking back to the jeep together and Jack enquired, "Who is going to be my copilot today?"

"You're looking at him, buddy," I answered.

Jack replied, "Now that is just peachy; you're gonna be my butt doctor *and* copilot, all in one day!"

Waldo chimed in, "Not only your butt doctor and copilot; you can bet that he is going to expand your knowledge of modern music to make our top-secret flight a bit more entertaining, in the face of oncoming danger. By the way, now that we've gotten to know each other a bit, you can call him Colonel Bubble Butt, or simply BB. You can call me Waldo. What is your nickname, Captain Smith?"

Jack replied, "Bucky; you can call me Bucky."

Waldo, BB, and Jack, AKA Bucky, walked back to the jeep, where Sergeant Darby Nelson was waiting. Jack said to Darby, "You and I are flying our mission with these guys and their crew today. Let's drive back to the barracks and tell our crew that they need to stand down, they will be staying here today."

Darby, who was British, replied, "They will be happy to stay home today, Bucky. Our mission is to bomb the Merseburg oil targets deep inside the Third Reich, including the Leuna synthetic oil refinery. Those guys are gonna say, 'See you later suckers, it's been nice knowin ya!'"

"Darby," Waldo interrupted, "being such a little smartass, what's your nickname?"

Darby who had an obvious British accent, answered, "Well, General, they call me 'Pumpkin' because my face is a bit round, and when I get embarrassed, I turn more orange than red." Waldo and I couldn't keep straight faces after that explanation, and started laughing uncontrollably.

Waldo, trying to regain his composure, said, "OK, Pumpkin; you and Bucky get back to the barracks and let the crew know to stand down. Give them a story to tell in case our mission goes bad, and then get your butts back here pronto. That's an order, we have a mission to fly!"

As Bucky and Pumpkin pulled away in their jeep, Waldo and I momentarily stared at each other, then gazed at our plane, named Bad Love. I scratched my head and said, "Well, that was interesting. It looks like we are go for launch; let's go prep the crew!"

Once on board, we proceeded to check on everyone and their stations. The crew was assigned to their positions as follows:

1. Pilot: Jack "Bucky" Smith
2. Copilot: Kevin "Bubble Butt" Schafer
3. Bombardier: Paul "Waldo" Thompson
4. Navigator: Darby "Pumpkin" Nelson
5. Radio Operator/Gunner: Billy "Willy" Blanchert
6. Ball Turret Gunner: Donny "The Runt" Legrand
7. Top Turret Gunner: Danny "Tater" Ford
8. Right Waist Gunner: Brianna "Cleopatra" Williams
9. Left Waist Gunner: Karen "Crisco" O'Sullivan
10. Tail Gunner: Frankie "Spaghetti Head" Russo

Everyone had changed into their A-2 leather flight jackets, boots, and headgear. We were also wearing Willy's Koss Phase-2 headphones, which were hooked into the plane's intercom system. Flight gloves, oxygen masks (the B-17G did not have a pressurized cabin), and flak vests were also ready to go. I walked to the cockpit and settled in to the copilot seat, then went through my initial preflight checklist. Next Willy and I got the intercom system working, in conjunction with the kick-ass Koss Phase-2 headphones. I wanted to give the Bad Love Crew a quick pep talk before Jack and Darby returned for our take-off.

I started by having everyone except Jack and Darby audibly check in. After hearing everyone's voice, I then spoke to the Bad Love Crew about our mission.

"Well, Bad Love Gang, this is what we prepared for during the past three months. Here we are, all together in a brand spanking new, 1944 B-17-G bomber we have named Bad Love, ready to go on our first time travel rescue mission! Just to remind you, we are flying first to bomb the Leuna synthetic oil refinery deep in Nazi Germany—and that is the *easy* part! After our bombing run, we are then continuing on to German-occupied, western Poland and landing near Chelmno. As you know, the Chelmno extermination camp is a wicked place that operates to execute Jews, Gypsies, and some Soviet prisoners of war. It is estimated that the total number executed there during this war was about three hundred forty thousand souls. At this moment in November of 1944, the only remaining active concentration camps are at Chelmno and Auschwitz, and Chelmno is winding down its operation to close in January 1945. Three days ago, we sent Goondoggy, Meatball, the Pud, and Crazy Ike to scout out the Chelmno area, rescue any Holocaust victims they could without getting caught, and find us a landing site in the rural countryside nearby. I have a surprise for the Nazis if they try to meet us at our landing and extraction site: Save some of your

50-caliber ammunition for that possibility, and if I tell you to man your battle stations while we are on the ground there, then get ready to unleash hell with all thirteen of those fifty-caliber machine guns! We will fly the folks we rescue to Belgium, land, and release them in Allied territory before we take off again and land at Kortenberg, Belgium—just in time for Bowmar to zap us back to the future, keeping the story of the Phantom Fortress intact. While we know that we can only rescue a few people from this horrific Holocaust, we have all agreed that the meaning and value of saving one single life is beyond measure; that is why we are here on this rescue mission."

I continued, "Aristotle said, 'Adventure is worthwhile.' All our lives, we have gone on amazing adventures together—but today takes the cake. So, if it is OK with all of you, we are going to make the most of this because, as our Bad Love Gang motto says..." All eight Bad Love members on board said in unison, "Live dangerously, have fun, don't die!"

Just as I finished, Jack and Darby returned. Jack parked their jeep, then both climbed aboard and quickly got dialed in with their flight gear and Koss headphones. "Say hi to our pilot, Jack 'Bucky' Smith, and our navigator, who can also double as a bombardier, Darby 'Pumpkin' Nelson," I announced.

Crisco and Cleopatra blurted out, nearly simultaneously, "Those are such cute names!"

Bucky nearly fell out of the pilot's seat. "This is no place for women! How's this gonna work?"

Cleopatra immediately responded, "Do you mean it's no place for a white woman, or no place for a black woman? 'Cause either way you pick, Bucky Boy, you can come right on back here for a little whoopass, you hear me? That goes for you too, Pumpkin!"

"I didn't say anything!" Pumpkin protested. "It's totally fine by me, I'll be your navigator eight days a week!"

Crisco added, "We are here to give new meaning to the name waist gunners; after this mission, they are going to rename this position hip gunners, after me and Cleopatra!"

Tater joined the banter in his typical southern drawl. He said, "Listen to me, Bucky; I recommend that you mind your own biscuits, and your life will be gravy."

I jumped in to end this chatter, "Well after that little bitch glitch, let's move on and have everyone else introduce themselves."

Crisco whispered to Cleopatra, "When we get a chance, we're gonna double-team BB and make him pay for that comment!"

"Yeah, baby," Cleopatra agreed.

We were scheduled to take off with ten other planes and fly high squadron in the group formation. It was 6:25 AM, and all the planes were warming up; Bucky and I quickly went to work. As we finished the preflight checklist, Bucky noticed my cassette player and tapes. "What is that little machine, BB?" he asked.

I replied, "That, Bucky, is the magic of modern music of the future! You are going to get your first dose of that future soon, through that state-of-the-art, 1974 headset you are wearing. I have to warn you, it will be radically new, and different than anything you have ever heard before. But you might find yourself enjoying it—we shall see. You can turn the volume up or down using the knob on the right earpiece. Just remember to keep flying the plane."

"BB, this plane is 1944 state-of-the-art, and she can just about fly herself. This amazing machine is gonna win your heart for sure!"

Bucky, watching the procession of planes, promptly said, "It's time to move it or lose it, BB!" I used the intercom to alert the crew.

"It's time to *light* this candle, boys and girls!" Bucky and I then fired up the engines one by one. As each engine snarled and coughed to life, white, grey, and black smoke blew back—and the engines were so magnificently loud! It was like a symphony of roaring power that filled the cabin of the B-17G, seemingly shaking both heaven and earth. *This is the definition of WWII Allied airpower,* I thought, and it made me feel proud that it was made in America.

Bucky got on the intercom to Frankie Russo, at the tail gunner position. "Hey Spaghetti Head, when we taxi over to our takeoff spot, I want you to lock the tail wheel into the fixed position." The tail wheel on the B-17 could rotate or be locked in place. The process of locking the B-17 tail wheel in place to takeoff or land made sense for straight-line stability. However, allowing it to rotate while making turns during taxiing also made sense, and I would remember this for future reference.

Frankie answered the call, "I may have short arms," referencing an Italian phrase used to describe someone as cheap, "but I can take care of the tail wheel, no problem!"

"We all know that we can bank on Frank!" I said.

Frankie shot back, "You bet your sweet ass, BB! Let's get this plane in the air!"

Bucky moved the throttles forward and Bad Love lurched ahead onto the feeder runway, following our squadron's line of planes. The tall grass fields at the edges of the runways where we had landed from our time travel, just a short time ago, were blowing like waves in the sea from the powerful four-engine bombers making their way to their takeoff runs. Before I knew it, we were lined up for takeoff.

As Bucky waited for the plane ahead of us to clear the runway, I plugged in the Marantz Superscope CS200 portable cassette player, making it ready to play on the general intercom. I also forewarned

Bucky that takeoff music would be playing for the entire crew, and that we would be having a 1960's and early 1970's musical tour de force before the call of duty took place. Despite our age difference, Bucky and I had started to bond; I definitely had his curiosity tweaked about this "modern music" thing. Plus, Waldo had already told Bucky that music was part of our mission. I told Bucky that our takeoff song was recorded in 1973, but released in January 1974—and still going strong in late 1974. Bucky looked at me and said, "Buckle up, Bubble Butt! Here we go!" He then simultaneously shoved the four throttles forward and stood on the brakes for a short bit. The four Wright Cyclone engines roared to power, then he released the brakes and we "shook, rattled and rolled" as we loudly thundered down the runway, like a giant bat out of hell. I instinctively hit the *play* button on the Marantz cassette, and the 1974 song by Bachman Turner Overdrive (BTO), **"Takin' Care of Business,"** filled the ears of the crew.

In every station of the plane the Bad Love gang (except for Pumpkin, who listened and started tapping his right foot) pretended that they had microphones in their hands, and lip synced the words of "Takin' Care of Business." Two-thirds down the runway we left the ground and met the sky, flying away from the East Anglia airbase. We headed east, out over the English countryside and toward the North Sea. Our takeoff into the destiny of time travel in a WWII B-17 named Bad Love was simultaneously surreal and real!

CHAPTER FIFTEEN

THE FUN PART OF THE FLIGHT

"I can't tell you what I had for breakfast,
but I can sing every single word of rock and roll."
—Patty Duke

P rior to the start of our mission, I had asked each member of the
Bad Love crew to pick a favorite road song or personal favorite; I
had also created a song list for our in-flight entertainment. Willy and I
had skillfully recorded all these songs onto cassette tapes to play on the
Marantz Superscope C200 that was now plugged into and integrated
with the general intercom system. All of us, minus Jack (Bucky) and
Darby (Pumpkin), were here from November of 1974, and grew up
with the music of the 1960s and early 1970s. We all loved the music of
our generation, and none of us were shy about singing, dancing and
turning up the volume.

As we watched the English countryside passing by us below and the
typically British grey, overcast sky around us, I went on the intercom
and asked the crew, "Are you guys ready for a little musical tour de
force?" At least seven voices shouted out in the affirmative. I asked,
"Any of you longing for home yet, on this cold, grey day? How about
a little Mamas and the Papas?" When I hit the play button, we were
immersed in the song **"California Dreamin'."**

Crisco and Cleopatra were swinging and swaying arm in arm, singing along at the waist gunner positions. The rest of the crew were staring out of their windows, also singing along. Willy blurted out, "I can remember seeing them for the first time on *The Ed Sullivan Show*, back in December 1966. Mama Cass couldn't keep her hair out of her eyes, and I kept blinking and rubbing my eyes while I was watching her on TV! I'm having a flashback now, trying to get the hair out of my eyes. And I have a military haircut!"

I asked, "Remember that sunny summer day when Crisco tried to teach us all how to do the twist in her front yard, and we all failed so miserably?"

In his Southern slang-filled accent Tater said, "It was hotter than a hooker's doorknob on payday, and I didn't want to get my feathers ruffled."

I was watching Bucky laugh to himself when the Runt added, "The only time that I can ever dance is waiting to use the bathroom: We only have one bathroom, and five kids. I'll be damned if I'm gonna pee or shit in my pants, so I start dancing! It works every time, but it ain't pretty."

I said, "Hey, everybody, you'll know that the Runt is prairie dogging it when you see him start to dance!" We all laughed, Crisco and Cleopatra with minimal eye rolling. I continued, "So Crisco picked out a song perfect to play as we start flying over the North Sea, which is now directly below us. Here we go with **'C'mon and Swim,'** by Bobby Freeman."

Crisco and Cleopatra were immediately doing the dance called the Swim, and nearly everyone headed to the back of the plane and joined in: Spaghetti Head, the Runt, Tater, Willy, and even Pumpkin gave it a try. Pumpkin stood and watched everyone for a minute, then he "jumped in the pool!" They were all pretending to swim or holding their noses with one hand, and holding their other hand up above their heads, waving it as if they were sinking into the pretend water.

We could still see the northeastern coast of England behind us. I said, "Before we totally leave sight of England, we have to play Willy's favorite song that he picked for this occasion, starring that fab four from Liverpool. You guys are aware that Willy acts much older than his stated age, so he is already thinking ahead about getting some help in his old age. You know what I mean: someone to help pull his pants up to his nipples, comb the hair he has left, and hand him his dentures in the morning."

Willy retorted, "Hey, Bubble Butt! Wipe your mouth; there is still a tiny bit of bullshit around your lips!"

Then I said, "Without further ado, I give you Willy's song: **'Help!'** by the Beatles."

There is nothing quite like singing a Beatles song if you grew up in the 1960s. You know all the words and the very sound of the music, because they are imprinted on your consciousness: branded in your brain. We were all singing and rockin' along, and I noticed Bucky getting into it for the first time. Bucky looked at me and said, "I kind of like this sound!"

I announced, "Bucky has now taken the musical time travel to the sixties and likes the Beatles, so there is hope in the modern world for our captain!"

As "Help!" faded out, I decided to switch gears again and knock on Cleopatra's door. "So, y'all, now we're going to check out Cleopatra's selection for today. She fashions herself as our 'diva divine to keep us in line'."

Cleopatra quickly cut me off. "Hey, Bubble Butt, everything that you do for attention is why you don't have mine."

I responded, "I'll get your attention real quick, because, as the Supremes say, **'You Keep Me Hanging On!'**" I hit the play button.

Cleopatra was instantly in her element, and so was I. The Supremes were my sisters' favorite group in the '60s, and we had every 45 RPM record they ever recorded. I had visions in my head of watching my two sisters and their friends dancing to the Supremes with our jukebox playing at home as I tried to sing along, in the highest pitched "female" voice that I could muster. Bucky looked at me like I was totally out of my mind, but I just smiled at him and kept singing! Cleopatra did her best impersonation of Diana Ross for everyone in the back of the plane, and they all danced along with her. When the music stopped, I got on the intercom for some trivia.

"OK, here are a few fun facts about Diana Ross and the Supremes. They have appeared on *The Ed Sullivan Show* twenty times, which is more than any other pop group in the history of that show. They have had twelve number one hits in the USA so far, but have not yet won a single Grammy."

Cleopatra got on her high horse for a moment, protesting, "BB, you're full of it! They have won tons of Grammys!"

I quickly replied, "OK, 'Your Wrongness,' you are entitled to your incorrect opinion!"

Cleo looked at Crisco and said, "BB is in so much trouble!"

We were still over the North Sea, and I turned our collective attention to Waldo. "Waldo did a pretty good job this morning passing as a two-star major general. That's what you get for being forty-three years old and having a prematurely advanced male balding pattern!"

Waldo calmly replied, "You got that right, Bald Butt. I'm like Telly Savalas, and you can call me Kojak." This was the name of a tough detective on a popular TV show called *Kojak*, in its second season in 1974. We had intermittently watched episodes at Waldo's house, mainly because it was one of Waldo's alter egos. "Everyone knows that bald men are stronger, smarter, and sexier. I have always told you boys and girls that 'Age and treachery will beat youth and talent every time!' Any time any of you little shits want to try me, well, bring it on!" That was so Waldo!

I dived back in, saying, "I asked Waldo to pick a song, too. As you would expect, he picked one about the many untrustworthy women he dealt with before finding his one and only, Mary. I give you **'She's Not There,'** by the Zombies."

Most of us sang along while we imagined the girl who called off her wedding weeks before her wedding day and broke her man's heart. Waldo came on the intercom to point out, "At least for an ol' fart, the song that I picked made it to number two on the charts in 1964."

Several voices came through the intercom to say, "That was a good pick, Waldo." Bucky said, "I salute you, General Waldo; even *I* liked that a lot!"

I knew that I could pep up the pace of the show a little bit by picking on Tater for a few moments. "So, what do y'all think Tater might have picked for the proverbial road?" I asked.

Everyone chimed in, "You can bet it's CCR!" We all knew that stood for Creedence Clearwater Revival, Tater's favorite group. Tater, who must have been daydreaming and in some kind of self-induced trance, woke up and came on the intercom. "All my buddies are girl crazy, but let me share some Southern wisdom with y'all: What doesn't kill you makes you stronger—except for country girls. Country girls will just kill you."

I said, "I'm not so sure where you're going with that, Tater, but here is Tater's favorite road song: **'Travelin' Band,'** by Creedence Clearwater Revival."

This song got us all rockin', big time! Everyone in the plane—except for me and Bucky, stuck in the pilot and copilot seats—was dancing in the aisles and pretending to sing along, lip syncing the words into their pretend microphones. I could have sworn I felt the big bomber bouncing a bit from everyone jumping around to this staple song of country rock and roll. Tater, in his thickest Southern accent, blurted out, "Well, butter my butt and call me a biscuit! Everyone here seems to be rather fond of my choice for a road song!"

Bucky asked, "What the hell is a seven thirty-seven comin' out of the sky?"

Willy, doing some quick math, quipped, "That would be the Boeing Aircraft Company's seven thirty-seven, two engine passenger jet: seven hundred twenty planes into the future." (B-737 minus B-17 equals 720).

Hardly anyone got Willy's joke, so I reverted back to CCR for a minute. "Tater's pick from CCR was one of a two-sided hit record that was released in January of 1970: 'Travelin' Band' and 'Who'll Stop the Rain.' Except for Elvis Presley, Ricky Nelson, the Everly Brothers, and the Beatles, Creedence Clearwater Revival has had more success with two-sided hit singles than any band up until now."

Bucky looked at me and said, "BB, I am literally trained for special ops, but I have to tell you that this mission is something different. Maybe 'crazy ops' or 'insane ops' would fit better."

"We may be crazy, but we are definitely on a rescue mission. I promise you that you will see that it fits the definition of *special ops*," I reassured him.

I had mine and two more of the crew's road song favorites to play, and the timing with our progress in the air was working out just fine. I started in on Donny "The Runt" Legrande next, saying, "Let's all give out a shout to our perfect fit of a ball turret gunner, who also juiced our four Wright Cyclone engines before we took off for extra power today—just like he juiced his minibike to get away from that crazy building superintendent when we were kids."

Waldo interrupted, "You all are still kids in my book!"

Frankie "Spaghetti Head" Russo joined in, using his best Mafioso impersonation. "Waldo, I think you're forgetting the number one

Italian rule: *respect*! Stand down, and let's hear about the Runt's pick."
"Hey, thanks, Spaghetti Head, that may be the first time you ever stuck up for me!" the Runt exclaimed.

Frankie answered, "Don't get used to it, Runt!"

I continued, "The Runt has two older sisters like me, and he seems to still favor the music of the late fifties and sixties from listening to his sisters' music growing up. But he surprised me for this adventure, and picked a song released in August 1972. What's more, how could any musical tour de force possibly be complete without a song from Elvis 'the Pelvis' Presley? So in honor of the Runt, here is **'Burning Love,'** by Elvis Presley."

For us, this song was just a little over two years old. All the words were fresh in our minds, so we were all singing it to the end. Pumpkin came on the intercom and in his British accent said, "I still don't get where you all came from, but I have to say that I think that I could get to like your brand of music."

I came on to announce that "Burning Love" had made it to number two on the charts in October of 1972, but Chuck Berry's naughty song "My Ding-A-Ling" kept it from hitting number one. I told Pumpkin, "You'll have to wait a little while, buddy, but at least you know the future is not boring!"

That left just me and Frankie "Spaghetti Head" Russo on the road trip play list. Looking at the two songs remaining, I made the executive decision to go ahead of Frankie with my song, and save his song for last. "I had a bit of a struggle picking out a song, because I have gazillions of favorites from growing up in a family that loves all kinds of music, and I'm a bit of a rocker wannabe. You all know how much I loved *The Man from U.N.C.L.E.* on TV, and I can't wait for the next James Bond movie to come out! So I picked a spy song to memorialize our first top-secret, time travel rescue mission, flying in this B17-G bomber we've named Bad Love. I give you **'Secret Agent Man,'** by Johnny Rivers."

We all had fun dancing and lip synching about our newfound secret agent status! Crisco was the first to speak as the music faded. "BB, that song keeps saying that 'odds are you won't live to see tomorrow.' Are you trying to send us some subtle message, or what?"

In my very best James Bond impersonation from the movie *Goldfinger* I replied, "You're a woman of many parts, Pussy; don't let danger stand in your way."

Everyone, including Crisco, was laughing. Bucky, red-faced, was again nearly falling out of the pilot's seat. Trying to act chivalrous without laughing, he asked, "Did you just use *that word* and call Crisco... *Pussy* just now?"

I replied, "Honor Blackman played the part of Pussy Galore, the famous Bond girl from the 1964 spy movie *Goldfinger*."

Bucky responded, "You mean to tell me that a movie star named Honor Blackman goes by the name Pussy Galore in an actual, big-screen movie?"

I answered, "Yes, of course; the future is full of surprises like that! Here, let me prove it to you." I had anticipated a Bond moment like this, so I played **"Goldfinger"** by Shirley Bassey.

I found myself daydreaming about my model Aston Martin DB5 from Corgi Toys, which had become the best-selling toy of 1964. The Aston Martin DB5 James Bond drove in the movie had wheel-destroying blades, inspired by *Ben-Hur*'s scythed chariots; .30-caliber machine guns; oil slick and smoke screen emitters; and of course, the famous ejector seat. It was totally radical for 1964! Most dads in the mid to late 1960s who had seen the movie *Goldfinger* would tell their kids that if they misbehaved, he might have to push the ejector button, and eject them from the car. I very much doubted that it ever had any lasting disciplinary effect on rowdy kids, but it did make the dads feel falsely empowered!

"Earth to Bubble Butt; come in, Bubble Butt," registered in my headphones and then in my brain. I came to and reported to the crew, "Sorry about that lapse of contact, but I was daydreaming about using all the gadgets on the James Bond Aston Martin. It may just come in handy later today, only this plane is a much bigger, badder beast!"

I then announced to the crew, "We have one more so-called road song to play, the one that Frankie 'Spaghetti Head' Russo picked for this trip. I saved it until last. What's up with your pick, Frankie?"

He quickly replied, "I figured that this time travel launch and our first time travel mission was a bit like the Apollo missions. Sinatra's 'Fly Me to the Moon,' released in 1964, was closely associated with the Apollo missions to the moon. Plus, Frank Sinatra and the Rat Pack are about all my parents ever play for music at our home; for sure they must have named me after him!"

Pumpkin came on the intercom. "Did I hear you say that we fly to the *moon?*"

Frankie answered, "That's right, Pumpkin. On July twenty-first, 1969, a guy named Neil Armstrong takes mankind's first step on the moon."

Pumpkin blurted out, "No shit, Sherlock!" then went quiet.

"With no further delay, here is Frank Sinatra singing **'Fly Me to the Moon,'**" I announced.

Listening to Sinatra, I closed my eyes and imagined looking at the Bad Love B-17G from the sky, slightly above, in front, and to the starboard side as we came through a bank of puffy clouds on an incredibly bright, brilliantly moonlit night, flying into the destiny of time travel... only it was still early in the day, and we were headed into danger.

CHAPTER SIXTEEN

THE DANGEROUS PART OF THE FLIGHT

"Everything you want is on the other side of fear."
—Jack Canfield

Despite our unconventional, music-centric entertainment and crazy, random glimpse into the future, Bucky and Pumpkin had diligently kept us on course; we had just crossed over the Netherlands into German airspace. In prior days, this crossing would have been the start of danger. Earlier (particularly throughout 1943) in the Allied Eighth Air Force bombing campaign over Germany, the German air force—known as the Luftwaffe—would be coming out to meet us as we flew into Germany, if not before. The two most effective and feared Luftwaffe fighter planes that routinely fought the B-17 bomber groups and wreaked havoc on bombing missions like this one were the Messerschmitt Me-109 and the Folk-Wulf 190. However, in 1944 the game had changed, because the Luftwaffe had become severely degraded by an effective combination of Allied success strategies.

In early 1944, three of the most fearsome American fighter planes, the Lockheed P-38 Lightning, the Republic P-47 Thunderbolt, and the North American P-51 Mustang (the latter two equipped with external fuel tanks extending their range) were able to accompany the B-17s all the way to their targets deep inside Germany, including Berlin. These fighters became the B-17's "little friends," or "peashooters." They inflicted heavy losses on the Luftwaffe fighter planes while protecting the bomber groups so they could do their damage to German targets with high-precision, daylight bombing. In late 1943 and early 1944, the Allied bombing campaign focused its efforts on the German Air Force aircraft industry, with effective results.

In early March 1944, with the help and protection of P-47 Thunderbolts and P-51 Mustangs, the B-17s of the U.S. Eighth Air Force made their debut in a group bombing mission over Berlin, the German capital city. In the first large airstrike on Berlin, we did not send a small expeditionary force of bombers; we sent a massive show of force, with 600 heavy bombers flying to drop destruction on Berlin. The bombing of Berlin continued until the end of the war, but was very intense until early May 1944.

In early May 1944, our bombing strategy became more focused on Germany's oil-production industry, which included oil refineries and synthetic oil plants. The strategy was smart; by smashing and reducing Germany's oil supply, the already weakened German Luftwaffe would be hurting for aviation fuel. The German army tanks and road transport network would suffer, and the German Navy activities would also be adversely affected. In other words, the German war machine ran on the heartbeat of oil, and we were out to induce some cardiac arrest!

With the Luftwaffe already degraded and no longer such a "serious and regular" threat to our relentless daylight bombing missions, the Germans moved heavy concentrations of antiaircraft guns to make rings of defense around their most valued oil production refineries and synthetic oil plants. By the time we flew our mission on November 21, 1944, the German Luftwaffe was conserving what fuel it did have for its fighter planes to engage our bombers over their targets, not as our bombers crossed into German airspace.

Therefore, our biggest threat this day came from concentrated collections of antiaircraft guns pointed skyward, aimed directly at us as we approached the target—including the notorious German 88mm and 105mm flak guns. These ground-based flak gun batteries tried to pinpoint our incoming B-17s by firing gun shells that were designed to burst in a sphere of destruction sixty yards in diameter in an effort to destroy us, their target. The explosion of these shells in the air was called flak. Flak was a fearsome adversary to WWII American aircrews, and devastated many allied bombers over Germany. The German 88mm and 105mm guns could project flak shells to altitudes of 20,000–31,000 feet, and could knock out an aircraft within thirty yards of the shell burst. However, the shrapnel from the explosion was still capable of inflicting serious damage for up to 200 yards.

Just nineteen days prior to our Bad Love mission, on November 2, 1944, the Eighth Air Force had sent 638 B-17 Flying Fortress bombers, escorted by 642 P-51 Mustang and P-38 Lightning fighters from their bases in England, to attack the synthetic oil refinery at Leuna, located a few miles from Merseburg, Germany. The Leuna refinery used the hydrogenation and Fischer-Tropsch processes to produce aviation fuel from coal. This was the most heavily defended target in all of Germany, surrounded by more than 1,700 88 mm and 105 mm anti-aircraft flak guns. During the November 2nd attack, the bombers were under intense anti-aircraft fire for eighteen minutes, and heavy fire for thirty minutes. They were also attacked by a record 700 *Luftwaffe* fighters. The Eighth Air Force lost 38 B-17 Flying Fortress bombers and 28 fighter planes that day, and 481 of the returning B-17 bombers were damaged. The Allied aircrews viewed a mission to bomb Leuna as perhaps the most dangerous assignment of the air war over Europe.

That explained why the normal crew of our plane readily stood down when Bucky and Pumpkin told them our plane was going on a secret mission. They knew that the bomber squadron was scheduled to hit the Leuna synthetic refinery, and that was going to be about as much fun as rolling in a cactus and showering in lemon juice.

I called Pumpkin to the cockpit to have a private meeting with me and Bucky. It was time to better explain the true nature of our secret mission, and exactly how we planned for it to unfold and succeed. "Bucky, Pumpkin, we purposely picked this particular B-17 bomber on this day in 1944 because during this mission, it gets damaged by heavy flak, loses an engine and power, falls out of formation with the bombing group, and has to limp to Belgium, where it loses power to a second engine. By actual historical accounts, the pilot then reported putting the plane on autopilot and the entire crew bailed out over Belgium. They were safely picked up by British ground troops and sent back to England."

Pumpkin commented, "That kind of thing happens, from time to time. Planes are always getting damaged, and choosing to have the crew bail out is sometimes the smart thing to do, rather than trying to ditch or land a damaged plane and risk crashing and killing the crew."

I continued, "You are exactly right, Pumpkin. But here is where the story takes a major twist of fate. After the crew bails out of this particular plane on this very day in history, the plane somehow spontaneously restarts its two failed engines, flies itself to a British Royal Airforce airbase in Kortenberg, Belgium, and makes a perfect three-point landing in a plowed field—with no one on board. One of the four engines is damaged at the end of the landing roll, but the other three continue to run until a British officer climbs on board and turns them off. There was no one on board when the British officer investigated the inside of the plane. The plane is a basically a ghost ship, and becomes famous in WWII aviation lore; it is known as the Phantom Fortress.

"So that is why I got sent back to this day!" Bucky exclaimed. "The white hole time travel mission planners knew what you know, and they must have had other plans for this plane on this day. As a trained B-17 special-ops pilot, I can tell you that the story of this plane restarting its two failed engines 'all by itself' after everyone bailed out and then flying directly to an Allied airbase and landing perfectly is just a fairytale! Who would believe that crock of shit?"

I answered, "Apparently that story has been generally accepted, because there was no other explanation. But now, my team and the two of you know the truth about this plane. So, here is what is *really* going to happen today, with this beautiful new plane on its third-ever mission, now designated as Bad Love. According to the actual mission reports from this day in history, there is solid cloud cover everywhere over the Leuna synthetic oil refinery, and our squadron drops their bomb loads from high altitude; the results of the bombing are unobserved because of the thick cloud cover. However, as you would expect, the antiaircraft flak attack is very heavy, and accurate enough to cause damage to this plane; this damage happened after this plane turned with the squadron to make the bomb run."

Bucky interrupted, "Look out the window, guys." The cloud cover was as thick as pea soup, and we were getting closer to the turning point for the bombing run.

I was starting to get a bit excited. "Bucky, this is where your skill set is critical. According to the filed reports, our plane takes its flak damage after turning with the rest of the group to make the bomb run. So, this is what we're going to do: Just before we get to the pivot point, you are going to report an engine power failure; we are going to lose altitude, then have to turn back and away from the rest of the group.

Don't worry; we are not going to waste our bomb load, or run from danger. Instead, we are going to lay low, behind the cover of the clouds, while the rest of the group drops their bombs using their instruments. They will be drawing most of the flak fire during their run, and once the entire bombing group turns for home, the German ground gunneries will think that the raid is done. Any German fighter planes still in the air will return to base to conserve their precious fuel. We'll give them about fifteen to twenty minutes, then we go to work. Pumpkin, I need you to navigate us through the clouds directly to the center of Leuna refinery; Bucky, you will drop us through the cloud cover to bomb Leuna by sight, so that we can blow the crap out of that refinery! They won't be expecting a lone plane after the bombing raid is well over; hopefully, they will think we are one of theirs—or a damaged plane looking to land. After we drop our bombs, we get back into the clouds and set our course for Chelmno, Poland, which is thirty-seven point five miles northeast of Lodz, the third largest city in Poland."

"We can do this...but it is dangerous, BB," Bucky weighed in. "Assuming that Pumpkin puts us right on top of the Leuna refinery, any kind of low-level bombing in a B-17 is risky, because we are such a large target for anyone on the ground with a gun pointed at us. The Germans have lots of guns that can fire at targets a thousand feet above the earth. That would include their basic infantry rifles, and pretty much all their machine guns. They also have twenty, thirty-seven, and forty-millimeter rapid-fire cannons available. Above twenty thousand feet, their options dwindle to their eighty-eight and one hundred five-millimeter flak cannons. Our best bet is to drop below the cloud cover right on target, which depends on Pumpkin's navigation skills, quickly drop our bomb load, and then immediately get back into the clouds to avoid being accurately targeted by ground fire—or hunted by any German fighters that might come after us."

Pumpkin had been listening intently. His British accent very pronounced, he said, "You guys don't know me that well, but navigation is second nature for me. For some reason, I am a natural-born navigator; I will get us right on top of that friggin' refinery, to shock the shit out of those bastards!"

I had to comment on his cockiness. "You're sounding a bit like pumpkin pie with whipped testosterone on top!"

Pumpkin continued, "I heard you say that after we drop our bomb load, we are then setting course for Chelmno, Poland, a bit northeast of Lodz. Why are we headed there?"

I answered, "That is the primary purpose of our mission today. We are making a short stop there to pick up the rest of our Bad Love team, as well as rescue some Jews and Gypsies from the holocaust. I will explain that part, and the rest of the mission, to you after we bomb Leuna and make it out of there."

Bucky told Pumpkin to get ready to re-chart our course to the Leuna refinery, and I spoke to the crew on the intercom. "Everyone should be ready at their guns now. Along with the rest of the squadron, we are about ten minutes to our scheduled turning point to make the bombing run on Leuna. As we have previously rehearsed, in five minutes we are shutting down the number three engine, radioing the squadron that we are having a power failure, and dropping out of formation to hide in the clouds while the rest of the squadron drops their bombs. We are expecting heavy flak, but hopefully we can avoid the damage that this plane was reported to have endured by turning away a few minutes early. We will make our own surprise bombing run, then head for Poland as planned. So look sharp, and call out any German fighters you see. Don't waste any ammunition; take measured short bursts of fire, and only if you have them squarely in your sights. We are going to need our fifty-caliber firepower available, in case we have trouble on the ground in Poland."

Just then, Willy shouted out, "Bandits at twelve o'clock high, coming for our formation; those are Me-109s!" For a split second, I thought about Willy and me as kids, saying the same thing while taking our model airplanes on pretend missions—only this time it was real, and bullets had started to fly. Willy, Tater, and Cleopatra fired on the incoming Me-109s, and reported that one had a smoking engine after the concentrated 50-caliber machine gun fire from Bad Love.

We could hear and see flak rounds bursting in the sky all around us. Bucky cut the number three engine, and the plane shuddered and slowed a bit. He radioed the lead plane and told them we had lost our number three engine, and we were losing power; we couldn't maintain altitude. We started fading down and away from the rest of the squadron, just as they were turning to make their bombing run. At that moment, there was a loud explosion below us and to the starboard (right) side, and a flash of light. It occurred to me that was probably the flak shot that reportedly hit near our bomb bay on this day in history, only this time we were in the process of turning away and to the left. The Runt reported, "That flak burst left a big hole in the starboard belly of the fuselage, about the size of my pecker!"

Crisco teased him, of course. "Hey Runt, we'll have to take a picture of that little bitty, teeny tiny flak hole when we land to document your manliness!"

The Runt responded, "Well, hopefully we don't get a flak hole the size of your ass, or we're going down!"

Waldo said loudly, "Children, mind your manners!" Under his breath, he added, "You little shits."

We lost sight of the rest of the squadron as we dropped several thousand feet into the thick clouds covering all of Merseburg, Germany, the surrounding area, and the Leuna synthetic oil refinery that day. As we were descending, Bucky radioed that we had dropped our bombs and were going to try to make it back to England, but would fly to Belgium if we had further engine trouble. We leveled off at 12,000 feet, took our oxygen masks off, and continued to monitor the squadron's radio transmissions as they proceeded to drop all their bombs. The squadron had to use instruments to drop their bombs; the targets were not visible, given the thick cloud cover and their high-altitude bombing run. The 88mm and 105mm flak was very heavy that day; most of the radio chatter coming from the squadron related to the dense flak, and maneuvering away from it. I told Pumpkin to make a note in the bomber's log book about the heavy flak. Soon all the squadron's bombs were away, and they made their turn to head back to England. It was an eerie feeling to know that our bomber squadron and fighter escorts were heading back to the safety of England while we were covertly circling in the thick clouds below them, getting ready to embark on a lone mission to surprise bomb the Leuna synthetic oil refinery, and then head to Poland to rescue some Holocaust victims.

We continued to circle in the clouds outside of Merseburg, and eventually all the flak fire stopped. The radio chatter from our squadron faded and stopped as well; we were on our own. During one of our circles away from Merseburg, Bucky tested the lower edge of the cloud cover, which was between 6,000 and 9,000 feet. We were carrying a load of twelve 500-pound bombs in two racks. Pumpkin went back to the bomb bay to make sure that the bombs were armed and ready. Then we heard Pumpkin say, "What the heck are you two doing back here?"

Tater's southern voice was the next one we heard on the intercom. "Me and our resident artist, Crisco, decided to paint a little welcome message on one of these here bombs headed for the Leuna refinery."

Nearly everyone simultaneously asked what message they painted. Crisco came on the intercom and answered, "I painted our Bad Love logo, with the caption, 'Now you know how it feels to be on the wrong team!'" The crew agreed, exclaiming, "You got *that* right, Crisco!"

Bucky said, "Everyone man your stations! I am turning toward the target. Pumpkin, you do your thing and tell me when to take us down on top of those bastards. Waldo, you get ready to drop those bombs on command!"

For once, there was no discussion from Waldo. He said, "Yes sir, with immense pleasure, sir!" We started the ride through the thick clouds toward the target and Bucky increased the power to all the Wright Cyclone engines. The clouds were so thick we couldn't really see a thing. As our speed picked up, so did the turbulence. The bumpiness of flying through the clouds caused problems for some of the crew. Cleopatra and Crisco were trying to stand at their waist gunner positions, but getting bounced around like rag dolls. Cleopatra came on the intercom and commented, "This may be a cool plane and all, but it needs better shock absorbers!" I replied, "Get used to it Cleo, this B-17 has big stiff wings, and all these clouds will make for a rough ride."

Tater commented, "Quit yer bitchin', Cleo! Pretend you are a rodeo queen instead of a glamour queen!"

Cleo shot back, "Listen Tater, I'm not really a bitch; I just play one in your life."

"Ouch!" Tater replied.

On the ground below at the Leuna oil refinery, the 14th Flak Division responsible for protecting Leuna had 28,000 German troops and even more support personnel. The refinery was encircled by two concentrated rings of antiaircraft guns, one outer, more peripheral ring and an inner ring closer to the main refinery structure. The Leuna refinery covered three square miles of land with 250 buildings, including decoy buildings. It was the most heavily defended industrial target in all of Germany. On clear days, only 29% of the bombs aimed at Leuna landed inside the gates of the refinery; on radar-targeted bombing raids like today, that number dropped to about 5%.

Standing at their inner ring, 88mm flak cannon position were two German soldiers, Dieter Hofmann and Hans Klein, smoking cigarettes and talking up a big story about various current German affairs and about how they had just "blown the living shit" out of the American B-17 bombers trying to bomb the Leuna refinery, about 20 minutes ago. The American bombs had widely missed the Leuna oil refinery, and the ground-based flak gunnery crews of the 14th Flak Division were relaxing, taking bathroom breaks and patting themselves on the backs for a job well done.

Dieter Hofmann was a big, older, overweight, unshaven, and generally scruffy-appearing gunnery sergeant who was cynical about the war and Germany's future. Hans Klein was a young, athletic-looking, idealistic gunnery corporal who had spent some time in the Hitler youth program (the Nazi version of the Boy Scouts) while growing up. Dieter, taking a big, deep draw from his freshly-lit cigarette, said, "Listen to me, boy; the Russian Army is closing in from the East; the British, Canadians and Americans are closing in from the West since they landed in Normandy in June. And those B-17s have been pounding the crap out of Berlin when they are not trying to bomb us here. I'm too old, too fat, and too tired to do anything else but try and defend this place. You, on the other hand, should get yourself a better life and get the hell out of here."

Hans, trying unsuccessfully to blow smoke rings and coughing a bit, cockily replied, "I am proud to fight for the Fuehrer and Fatherland! I know that just as we beat away those American bombers this morning, Germany will never fail and never surrender!"

Dieter commented, "We may not get the luxury of surrendering, my little German strudel."

Just as they each lit another cigarette, Hans said, "Dieter, do you hear the sound of an approaching plane?" At first, Dieter couldn't hear it; years of gunnery work had affected his baseline hearing ability. Then the engine noise started to grow louder, and Dieter looked hard at the low, heavy cloud cover. "It must be a small squadron of our fighter planes returning from chasing those American bastards away," he suggested hopefully. The engine noise coming from four Wright Cyclone, B-17G engines running at full throttle, with the Runt's magic fuel mixture adding more power, got noticeably stronger; the local earth started to shake. Hans Klein didn't realize he was speaking his final words when he loudly proclaimed, "Our German airplanes are the strongest and finest in the world. Listen to the power of those engines!"

Just then, 6,000 feet above them, a gleaming, new American B-17G bomber rapidly came down out of the thick cloud cover and in a perfect line of sight through their position into the center of the main complex, dropped its load of a dozen 500-pound bombs. The two men's eyes were wide open, their faces frozen in confusion and fear; their cigarettes dropped from their mouths, and for a brief second, they recognized it was a lone American B-17 bomber coming directly at them at high speed. The first bomb to explode turned Dieter, Hans, and their gun position into a molten, bright light of exploding destruction, sending them rapidly into the next life.

Seconds before, aboard Bad Love with the bomb bay doors open and the 6,000-pound bomb load armed and ready, Pumpkin had told Bucky to throttle up to full power and descend quickly to between

5,000 and 6,000 feet. The inside of the plane was magnificently loud from the roar of the engines at full throttle. Every crew member on Bad Love had their adrenalin rushing and eyes peeled for the ground, examining the area for the Leuna Oil Refinery. Pumpkin was perfectly on target. We looked on with amazement as we came down through the clouds, and saw directly ahead through our pilot's windshield and out our plexiglass nose. Perfectly aligned with the central core of buildings in the complex known as the Leuna oil refinery, we were approaching them at an airspeed of 275 MPH. At that moment, Pumpkin literally yelled, "HOLY *SHIT*, WALDO! BOMBS AWAY!" Waldo did not blink an eye; he immediately released the entire bomb load. A total of twelve 500-pound bombs sequentially fell in a line, ripping through the center of the Leuna oil refinery complex.

The initial explosions actually rocked Bad Love in the sky and created complete pandemonium and confusion throughout the Leuna Refinery Complex below. But what happened next in rapid succession was nothing less than spectacular. Several of the bombs happened to hit high octane, synthetic aviation fuel lines leading to above and below ground storage units, the expansive explosions creating large fireballs within the complex that shot more than a thousand feet in every direction, including skyward. Buildings and pipelines blew apart, with large objects flying randomly in a beautiful, moving portrait of destruction wrought by B-17 firepower. We were all trying to watch the fireworks; Pumpkin yelled at Bucky to pull up into the low cloud cover just as fast as we had made our brief but deadly appearance.

Antiaircraft guns did erupt from the peripheral ring of defense, and we could see glimpses of their muzzle flashes as we climbed back into the dense cloud cover. Frankie "Spaghetti Head" Russo was still in his tail gunner position, and spoke on the intercom. "There is a great Mafia saying for those poor bastards down there, at this moment." He paused, and we were all waiting for him to say something profound. Then he said, "Nothing personal, it's just business!" Frankie had a birds-eye view of our bombing results out the back of the plane from his tail gunner position, and had the final look before we went back into the protective cloud cover. He was excellent at calculating percentages, particularly when it came to destruction. He then continued, "I would estimate that we just shuttered about thirty-three percent of Leuna's production with that direct hit. We were in and out of there so fast and so unexpectedly that the antiaircraft fire from the periphery got started late. The secondary explosions threw everyone off, and the return fire looked to be well behind us."

We were quickly back to flying the bumpy rodeo in the sky within the heavy cloud cover over Eastern Germany, and Pumpkin had us on an easterly course heading to Chelmno, Poland. I got on the intercom to announce, "We have less than a two-hour flight time to Chelmno, where we will be looking to make radio contact with the Pud, Crazy Ike, Meatball, and Goondoggy. Say your prayers for this critical part of our mission. Hopefully, they have identified a suitable landing spot where we can scoop them up, and rescue any Holocaust victims they have found. We are now six thousand pounds lighter after dropping our bombs on Leuna; we can take on some human cargo, no problem. Our plan is to minimize our time on the ground there. It is Nazi-occupied Poland, and you can bet they won't appreciate our rescue visit. It is a good thing that you saved most of your fifty-caliber ammunition. I have a suspicion that we will need it!"

CHAPTER SEVENTEEN

THE MOST DANGEROUS PART OF THE FLIGHT

"In these days of difficulty, we Americans everywhere must and shall choose the path of social justice...the path of faith, the path of hope, and the path of love toward our fellow man."
—Franklin D. Roosevelt

B ucky was getting a world-class workout handling the turbulence at the pilot's controls as we continued through the clouds toward Poland. "Where did your Bad Love gang come up with all these hilarious nicknames?" he asked.

"I guess we were pretty creative as little kids growing up—or maybe I should say we were creatively mean!" I then called Pumpkin back up to the cockpit so he, Bucky, and I could review the remaining mission parameters ahead of us. Before I could get started, Pumpkin spoke.

"So, Bubble Bath...I mean, Bubble *Butt*, I kind of like working with this crew—a lot. This mission is by far the most fun that I have had in the war, despite the crazy danger we have faced along the way. I was adopted, do not have a wife or steady girlfriend, and both my adoptive parents were killed last year in a night-time Nazi bombing raid on London. I would not be too missed if I disappeared in action. If you and your lofty ideas, your music, and the Bad Love gang are the future, then I'd like to be a part of it. I want to travel back to the future with you guys."

As Pumpkin made his case, I thought to myself what an asset he had been on our mission, and what a natural fit he seemed to be with the rest of us. As a person, you just couldn't help but like him, his attitude, and his British accent and background. Pumpkin had literally navigated us through thick clouds to come out right on top of the Leuna refinery, perfectly positioned for a direct hit on our bombing run. It was nothing less than spectacular, really. I was also musing about what missions we might try later on, and thinking that having his skill set would complement our group talent even more. Not only that, I just couldn't wait to have Crisco and Cleopatra embarrass him in some silly way, so that we could see his face blush whatever shade of orange gave him his nickname!

Looking Pumpkin in the eye, I got on the intercom to Willy. "Hey, Willy, how many extra implantable GCPDs did we bring with us?"

Willy replied, "We determined that the white hole time machine could transport a maximum of fifteen persons at one time. We launched Goondoggy, Meatball, Crazy Ike, and the Pud to Chelmno three days ago; then we launched the eight of us to get this plane in England this morning. That is twelve time-travel slots accounted for, and I brought three extra GCPDs with us in case any got damaged—or we decided we had to bring someone back with us. Bowmar is planning to use all fifteen return GCPDs as part of our backup plan when he zaps us back to 1974 later today."

I already knew that Bucky was coming back with us, so that left two more global cosmic positioning devices (GCPDs) in reserve. "Attention all Bad Love crew members," I announced over the general intercom. "It seems that Pumpkin is having too much fun for one day! He wants to join our crazy gang and come back to the future with us. We do have an extra GCPD device that he could use. I think that it is one of those bulky prototype models, so I am going to have to make an extra-large incision in his buttocks to get that thing in there!" Pumpkin immediately looked scared, and turned pale. "That was just a joke, Pumpkin," I said, and everyone laughed. "So, let's have a vote about Pumpkin joining the Bad Love Gang and going back to 1974 with us."

Cleopatra came on and seductively said, "Hey, Pumpkin baby... I have to teach you how to dance and romance '70's style if you're coming back with me–I mean, *us!*" Several cries of, "Whoa, you *go*, girl!" rang out, and Pumpkin's face actually did turn a shade of orange, which I immediately told the crew looked like Tang: the powdered "space-age" drink inspired by NASA. Everyone voted affirmative and I said to Pumpkin, "It looks like you and Bucky both are headed back to 1974 when we land this plane in Kortenberg, Belgium later this afternoon."

We needed to refocus on the mission, so I reviewed our plans. "OK Pumpkin, now that we have that issue settled, let's talk about the rest of our day. We are on a course to Chelmno, Poland to rendezvous with the rest of our Bad Love gang: Goondoggy, the Pud, Crazy Ike, and Meatball. Three days ago, we used the white hole time machine to transport the four of them there on November 18, 1944. Their mission was to rescue Jews and Gypsies who are scheduled or destined to be exterminated at the Chelmno death camp. As of this moment in history, Chelmno and Auschwitz are the only two Holocaust extermination camps still in operation. The Chelmno operation typically killed a thousand victims per day earlier in the war; now, in November 1944, the operation is winding down, with about ten thousand victims killed so far this year. Our goal is to rescue who we can on this day, with the philosophy that there is no price or value that can be placed on a single life—and even one Holocaust life saved will make this mission a complete success."

Pumpkin's eyes started to well up a bit, but Bucky quickly said, "This is no time for getting sentimental, Pumpkin; we have a mission to execute. I like the plan, but where are we going to land this big bird so we can pick up your crew and the folks they managed to rescue? It's not like there is a well-groomed airfield waiting to welcome us at Chelmno!"

I responded, "You know what, Bucky? You read my mind just now, because that is the next critical piece of this mission puzzle. We do need to find a suitable landing zone somewhere in the general vicinity of Chelmno, Poland. We have Gary 'the Pud' Jacobson on the ground there now, and his main job the last three days has been to find us a landing zone, and to be looking and listening for us today at high noon! The Pud is dialed in to communicate with us through our VHF transmitter-receiver radio set, and we should have good two-way radio communication with him when we get within a one-hundred-mile radius. In addition, I told him to build a smoky fire to mark the landing zone location as well, if at all possible."

Bucky responded, "You're telling me that we are depending on some guy you call the *Pud* to get us safely on the ground?"

I said, "He is a guy who is obsessed with all the little details. He will make sure that we have a long enough and flat enough landing zone, with no holes to ruin our landing gear. He earned his nickname when we were little kids for being the slowest, the last-place performer in our gang to run, jump, climb, or arm wrestle: hence the nickname the Pud. Now that we are teenagers, he is starting to come around; he has been getting a lot bigger and stronger, and he even lettered in varsity football this year. Pretty soon, we'll be calling him *Sir* Pud!"

Bucky commented, "You guys were terrible as kids, but I guess it made you all tough enough to travel through time. We need the Pud to put on his Sir Pud A-game to make this landing, rescue pick up, and quick takeoff escape plan feasible, especially using this big-ass B-17G as the vehicle."

I continued reviewing the plan. "Once we land, we need to roll to the end of the landing zone, where we will scoop up the Pud, Meatball, Goondoggy, Crazy Ike, and the holocaust victims they have rescued. When everyone is on board, we need to make like an egg and beat it, or make like a tree and leave."

Bucky looked at me with a roll of his eyes and said, "Maybe you should take a long walk off a short dock, BB!"

"On the ground, is it possible to stand on the left side brakes, fire the engines on the right wing, and spin the plane in a counterclockwise circle?" I asked Bucky.

He replied, "I have never tried it, but in theory yes, provided the tail wheel is unlocked so it can rotate—and you would probably have to pump the left brake, so that the wheel is not totally locked down, to allow it to roll and rotate a bit as well. Why would you ask a question like that?"

I replied, "It's my imagination asking what-if questions, that's all."

I turned my gaze to Pumpkin, explaining, "After we take off from Chelmno, Pumpkin, you'll need to plot a course to Chièvres Airfield in Belgium. In early September, Allied troops recaptured that base from the Germans and assumed command. Chièvres had been beat to shit by numerous Allied air attacks while it was held by the Germans, and it was further blown up and damaged by the Germans as they left. The combat engineers have repaired the damage to the airfield, and it was declared operationally ready for allied combat units in mid-September. Since October, P-47D Thunderbolts of the U.S. Ninth

Air Force and Eighth Air Force P-51 Mustangs have been stationed at Chièvres. The runway there is over six thousand, five hundred feet. We will land there and release all of our rescued Holocaust victims from Chelmno; Waldo will show our orders and explain that we are on a secret mission. While we are on the ground there, I have to implant the GCPDs in both of your butt cheeks. I have a perfectly sharpened, genuine American Bowie knife in the back of the plane, all ready to go for that surgical procedure; you guys can bite on fifty-caliber bullets while I do my dirty work! Maybe I'll play some music for you, to take your minds off the pain!" Pumpkin turned white again, and Bucky flipped me off.

I finished detailing the plan. "We will take-off from Chièvres and then fly to our final destination at the British Royal Airforce base near Kortenberg, Belgium. This part is a bit tricky; we need to touch down near the antiaircraft unit there at four PM local time, because that is precisely when Bowmar is bringing all fourteen of us forward in time to this day in 1974."

Pumpkin looked at me and said, "I'll get the courses plotted from Chelmno, Poland to Chièvres, Belgium, and from there to Kortenberg—but right now, you better fire up that VHF radio and start yakking for your buddy the Pud, and hope that he is ready for us, because we are almost there!

Bucky and I had been trading the flight controls back and forth for a while to give Bucky some much-deserved rest. Bucky got the VHF radio online, and we began hailing the Pud. "This is Bad Love One, this is Bad Love One, come in Pud! Come in Pud, throw us a line!" As we approached Chelmno by line of sight at about 11:10 AM, we saw smoke arising from a field that ended at the edge of a wooded area, and we aimed for that site.

At 11:16 AM, our VHF radio barked out, "Bad Love One, this is the Pud, do you read me?" I was overcome with emotion; I was so relieved, I actually started to cry a bit. I immediately patched in the general intercom and we all heard him say again, "Bad Love One, this the Pud, do you read me?" Everyone on board screamed and jumped with joy.

"Yes, we read you, Pud: loud and clear! This is Bubble Butt...over!"

The Pud responded, "Hey, Moon Butt! I mean, Bubble Butt! What took you guys so long? It's not like you've been out there fighting a war, or anything."

Bucky looked at me, smiling, and said, "Even though his name is the Pud, he's a grade-A smartass, just like the rest of you guys."

The Pud continued, "I have a small smoky fire burning where you need to taxi to, when you land. I have marked the center line of your grassy runway using some branches with bushy greenery. The runway is about four thousand feet, give or take. I have ensured that there are no hidden holes to hurt the landing gear—but it's a farmer's field, not a concrete runway. Approach from the south and land headed north-east. Guide the nose of the plane over the line of branches all the way back to where I am standing, next to the smoky fire. There is forest on all sides back here, except your runway in and out of here. To get back out of here, you have to get your ass turned around as you get close to the fire."

"What is the status of the rest of the team there?" I asked.

"Well, BB, it has been interesting. We have rescued thirteen souls from certain death at the Chelmno camp. Meatball is en route with all of them in the truck that we stole, and should be here any minute. Meatball fell in love with a Jewish girl named Hannah Lieb that we rescued, and I don't know how we are gonna pry the two of them apart! Goondoggy and Crazy Ike are nearby, hiding on either side of your makeshift runway and watching for the Nazis to show up. We stole the truck two days ago, and took the driver and guard as our prisoners. We hid in a summer cottage, and left there just a while ago to meet you here. Goondoggy and Crazy Ike are both riding stolen motorcycles, just like the good old days. The three of us got here first in case you were early...which you are, by about fifteen minutes. You can bet that the Nazis will see your unmistakably American, B-17 bomber landing, and be heading here like flies toward shit. So keep those Wright Cyclone engines fired up, make your turn to head back out, and we'll get everyone on board Bad Love faster than beans go through a cowboy!"

While we were talking, Bucky had circled south and west of the smoky fire marker. We could see the path of the makeshift runway to the northeast. He started our landing approach, and I lowered the flaps.

I got on the intercom and reported, "OK, Bad Love crew, this is it! We are landing in Poland to pick up the rest of our team and the thirteen souls we are rescuing from the Holocaust. It's going to be a bit of a tight fit getting everyone on board, but just do it, do it *quickly*, and stand ready to use your guns the minute we are fired upon. We are expecting trouble because, well, we *are* landing here in Nazi-occupied Poland in broad daylight, in a plane they call a fortress for a reason. Get everyone down on the floor to minimize the risk of taking bullets. Cleopatra and Crisco, put on your flak vests. Spaghetti Head, you need to unlock the tailwheel as we get to the end of our makeshift runway so that we can pivot and turn right away. Once we make the turn to head back out of here, get that rear hatch open as soon as we stop and get everyone on board. We'll have you lock the tailwheel again when we take off. Any questions?"

Tater, in his best country twang, asked, "How many Nazis does it take to screw in a light bulb?"

We all cried, "Tell us Tater!"

"None! They've already screwed up everything!"

During Tater's joke, the local German enlisted soldiers and Nazi SS soldiers assigned to Chelmno were galvanized into motion upon seeing an American B-17 coming in for a landing. The local garrison was not large or particularly ready for a ground battle, but those who were ready and available were closing in on our landing zone on motorcycles, staff cars, and trucks. Not much more than ten minutes behind Meatball was a German truck driven by Nazi SS sergeant Karl Becker, accompanied by privates Werner Koch and Manfred Weber. They were all young, and had been assigned to Chelmno in late August 1944 mainly to systematically burn and destroy Chelmno's installations: an attempt to erase all traces of the camp and kill the last few unfortunate Jews and Gypsies to be captured in the Holocaust era.

On Tuesday morning, November 21st 1944, Becker, Koch, and Weber had been following a lead that some strangers had been staying in a summer cottage in the countryside near Chelmno, reported by a neighbor walking his dog. They were hoping to find the truck and Jewish prisoners that unexpectedly disappeared on November 19th. They had arrived at the cottage about fifteen minutes after Meatball had departed. The nosey neighbor pointed in the direction that Meatball was headed. As they were driving in that direction, they saw the B-17 approaching to land and noticed the Pud's smoky fire. They had turned off the main road and were making their turn onto the same dusty, winding, country road that led to the back of the landing zone.

Becker had a machine gun and privates Koch and Weber had rifles, but they were not heavily armed. Weber looked at the other two and observed, "We are chasing the stolen truck with Jews and Gypsies, and an American B-17 is landing or crash-landing here. Do you think the B-17 is lost and has run out of fuel, or what?"

Becker, who was the ranking member of the three, responded, "There is no logical reason for an American B-17 to be coming to Chelmno, Poland. And whoever stole that truck with the Jews and Gypsies is heading in their direction. Get ready to shoot first and ask questions later, because I have a bad feeling about all this!"

As we were making our final approach, Meatball pulled up in the stolen truck with our thirteen souls to rescue. He parked the truck at the wooded end of the landing zone just as the Pud got busy extinguishing his smoky little fire by shoveling dirt on it. From the cockpit as we approached to land, I could see the thirteen rescued people getting out of the back of the truck, along with the two temporary prisoners (Aleksander Piontek and Jakub Nowak), who were escorted aside and seated in the rear corner of the landing zone. I saw two people emerging on motorcycles from each side of the forest, roaring onto the makeshift runway, and recognized them as Goondoggy and Crazy Ike. They appeared to be in a big hurry. Shivers ran down my spine as I thought *our Bad Love gang from November 1974 is all together here, in Poland, near the Chelmno extermination camp in November 1944, having been transported here for this rescue mission by the White Hole Project time machine! How bizarre!*

But it was real.

Unbeknown to those of us on Bad Love, the reason that Goondoggy and Crazy Ike were gunning it across the field on their motorcycles was to warn the Pud and Meatball that the Germans had finally caught up with them. They had seen the B-17 approaching to land, and they were closing in from both sides of the forest, racing toward our landing zone. Meatball looked back with his binoculars and could see a swastika-marked truck in the distance, coming from the same curvy dusty road that he had used to get to the back of the landing zone. Trouble was coming from all directions, and we had to move fast. The Pud's voice, now sounding panicked, shouted from our VHF radio, "*Move your asses!* BB, we will have big trouble here in just a few minutes!*"

And with that said, we came in to land, lined up with the guiding line of branches laid out in our landing field by the Pud, Crazy Ike, and Goondoggy. I found myself subconsciously counting down the feet to our touchdown, but I was also helping Bucky and going through the motions of the landing with him. We smoothly touched down and bounced a few times with room to spare as we quickly taxied right up to the Pud, Meatball, and our thirteen rescued folks at our turnaround point. Spaghetti Head quickly unlocked the rear wheel and we made our circle to point back to the way we had come in, set up for the takeoff. Goondoggy and Crazy Ike came barreling in fast on their motorcycles, locking their rear wheels and spinning around, then jumping off as the bikes skidded away from them—just like home, only they didn't care at all about any damage to these motorcycles.

Leaving Bucky in the cockpit, I went down to help get everyone on board. I climbed out the hatch on the front left side, below the cockpit, and yelled at Goondoggy, Crazy Ike, and the Pud to get on the plane using that entrance. We quickly hugged and high fived as they went by me to climb on board. As he passed by, Crazy Ike said, "BB, we need to bust our balls and get the hell out of here *now*. The Germans are hot on our trail!" Crazy Ike looked worried, which was rare, so I took that look as a strong signal to hurry up! I went to the back of the plane, where Crisco and Cleopatra had opened the rear entrance hatch and were assisting people boarding; Meatball was helping from outside the plane. Daniel and Mazal Roth, their daughters Zelda and Rhoda, and Mazal's mother, Rachel Soros, were the first of our rescued group to get on board Bad Love. I gave Meatball a big hug and jumped in to help. It was a bit windy and loud back there; the four Wright Cyclone engines were idling, standing ready to get us all back in the air. I yelled over the engine noise, "We'll get to meet each other once we are safely in the air, but right now you all need to *move* your butts, and get on board fast!"

The next two to get on board were Vadoma Loveridge and her son Barsali. Vadoma looked me in the eyes and pinched my cheek as she climbed through the hatch. She said, "I like you, future boy!" I might have blushed, but I was too busy focusing on getting everyone on board quickly. Benzion (Ben) Kaplan, the eight-year-old orphan boy (looking super excited to be flying for the first time) was next, followed by the older couple, Asher and Avigail Goldberg. Avigail, as would be expected at her age, was a bit slow getting through the hatch; I decided to push on her rump to help her move a bit faster. Rather than slap my hand, she looked back at me as she popped through the entrance.

"BB, you bad boy! I haven't been touched like that since Asher and I first met!" she exclaimed.

David, Sarah, and Hannah Lieb were the last three of our rescued group to board. David grabbed my hand and shoulder as Sarah was going through the hatch and said, "I am eternally indebted to you and your crew, you will never know the depth of my thankfulness."

I smiled and replied, "It means just as much to us, and you are welcome!" As David half-turned to get on the plane, I looked back to my right only to see Meatball and Hannah embraced in a major league kiss, like they had been dating for a long time. She was stunningly pretty, and I guessed a little bit older than Meatball.

Cleopatra saw this happening and yelled out, "Hey Meatball and Mrs. Jones!" (She referenced Billy Paul's 1972 hit song **"Me and Mrs. Jones."**) "I know you two got a thing going on, but you need to get inside this plane! *Now*, baby!"

Ushering them onto the plane, I teased, "Hannah, I mean 'Mrs. Jones', what are you doing robbing the cradle? And Meatball, you're a bigger stud than I ever realized!" Meatball tried to punch me, but swung and missed as he went through the hatch, which I shut and locked.

I turned to look back and saw the swastika-marked truck approaching fast on the curvy, dusty road behind us. I rushed to the back, jumped up and down knocking on Spaghetti Head's rear gunner window, and pointed to the approaching truck, which was in his field of view. I could see Frankie's acknowledgement, so I ran back to the left front hatch. As I got there, I scanned the area and saw vehicles coming from the right and left of our current position and runway out. There were not any tanks, heavy armored vehicles or halftracks at least, just a lot of staff cars, trucks, and few motorcycles headed in our direction. The Germans were on to us, and it was past time to get the hell out of there!

I ascended through the front hatch effortlessly, with adrenalin rushing through my body like never before; even though I was moving fast, the whole world around me seemed like it was in slow motion. I saw Goondoggy as I came on board, and told him to man the single 50-caliber machine gun to the left of Waldo, in the front near the Plexiglas nose, while Waldo operated the remote-controlled Bendix turret. I already knew that we were going to have to shoot our way out of here.

Just as I came to the cockpit, a bullet shot right through the left side of the cockpit window. Before I could say anything, Bucky slumped over the pilot's wheel with blood rolling down his forehead. I instinctively pulled him by his shoulders out of the pilot seat like I was Superman, strong with all that adrenalin pumping in my system. I laid him on the floor of the cockpit, behind the pilot and copilot seats. I yelled for Willy, who was actually just behind me. I said, "Willy, I am now the pilot, and you are my copilot!" Just then I heard 50-caliber machine gun fire from the rear of the plane. Frankie, "Spaghetti Head" Russo, at the tail gunner position, was the first of the Bad Love Gang to open fire with his dual 50-caliber machine guns, aiming at the truck driven by

Nazi Sergeant Karl Becker. They had gotten too close behind us on the dusty road approaching our position. Frankie put a burst of 50-caliber bullets into the front engine compartment of the truck carrying Becker, Koch, and Weber. The engine basically blew apart; the truck flew front first into the air while Becker, Koch, and Weber did their best to jump clear.

I was now in the pilot's seat, trying to keep my head down while putting my headgear on. Willy sat in the copilot seat and said, "BB, we are being surrounded! There are German vehicles on our right and left, and more on the way!"

I semi-yelled over the intercom, "Bucky's down! Crisco, get up here and attend to Bucky; Crazy Ike, take Crisco's waist gunner position. Everyone man your battle stations, and get ready to unleash hell on these Nazi bastards! I am going to stand on the left landing gear brakes, fire engines three and four on the right wing, and swing us in a full circle while all of you light up those woods, with every one of our thirteen 50-caliber machine guns blazing. Take out every vehicle you see as we swing around. Those 50-calibers will destroy anything they hit; they can chop down small trees to fall on the enemy. As we come out of this circle maneuver, we are headed down the runway to take off. Frankie, lock the tail wheel in place after we finish our circle, and the rest of you keep firing into the woods on either side of us as we make our way out of here. Waldo, if anyone tries to come in to block our exit after we start our takeoff run, blow the crap out of them using our chin turret before they get in our way. Make sure our rescued people are on the floor back there. Here we go!"

I initially stood on the left landing gear brakes and throttled up engines three and four. After we were turning in the circle, I pumped the left landing gear brakes and let the left tire move a little bit. Thank God, the left landing gear held up through the maneuver. Bad Love pivoted in a counter-clockwise circle as gale-force winds blew back from engines three and four; all thirteen of Bad Love's 50-caliber machine guns simultaneously fired on the enemy in the woods all around us. While I still don't know if any B-17 Flying Fortress was ever before used in a ground battle, it was a hell of a sight to see; fire blazed out of the barrels of all our guns, decimating the German vehicles. There were numerous small explosions from gas tanks being hit, while small trees and a multitude of tree branches fell on the enemy soldiers who made it out of their vehicles, diving onto the ground with their faces down. The circular wall of high-speed lead that we created as we pivoted in a circle prevented anyone from effectively firing on us.

As we completed the circle maneuver, I released the left landing brakes, throttled up engines one and two on the left wing, and yelled into the intercom, "NOW, Frankie! Lock the tailwheel! And Runt, these engines better run strong!"

The Runt replied, "Floor it, BB, and you'll see another miracle of raw power!" As I forcefully shoved all four engine throttles forward, the noise vibrated throughout the plane: a mighty mixture of thirteen 50-caliber machine guns blazing and four Wright Cyclone engines roaring up to speed. I was focused down the runway, but saw that to my left a German truck was heading out of the woods with a trajectory to block our takeoff. I yelled over the intercom, "Waldo, Goondoggy, bandit truck at ten o'clock; take that son of a bitch out *now!*"

Waldo immediately swung the remote-control Bendix chin turret around and opened fire with his twin 50-calibers on that truck. Goon-doggy did the same with the single 50-caliber gun on the left front. Three 50-caliber Browning machine guns were trained on the truck wanting to block our way out; Waldo aimed at the truck's engine compartment, and Goondoggy went for the driver and fuel tank. It looked like the Fourth of July in broad daylight when that truck blew to smithereens, flames and debris flying as it stopped dead in its tracks.

At almost the same time, a Nazi on a motorcycle came out of the woods from behind us to our right, trying to shoot at us with his left hand and drive the motorcycle with his right. We were halfway down the runway at this point, and gaining speed fast. Cleopatra was the first to see this crazed Nazi from her waist gunner position, and she took aim at the motorcycle. She basically walked a line of 50-caliber bullets across the field in front of that motorcycle, then right into it. It was no match for her aim. The motorcycle fell to pieces and the rider went flying, bouncing a few times over the field. On the intercom, Cleopatra commented, "I bet that Nazi is gonna have a tough time persecuting any more innocent people while he's wearing a full body cast!"

We were nearing the end of the makeshift runway at 125 MPH; I had purposely put on a little extra speed, since it was not a hard surface. I glanced at Willy who had our flaps down halfway, and said, "It's now or never, Willy; let's fly this thing!" With that, I pulled the wheel back hard. We left Chelmno, Poland behind and headed skyward, giddy with relief. Everyone on Bad Love started to cheer, whooping and hollering.

Looking back from his tail gunner position, Frankie got on the intercom again with his second damage report of the day. He exclaimed, "It's basically total destruction down there! I can see lots of wrecked, smoking vehicles. The woods are smoking too; looks like they're on fire as well!" Also for the second time that day, he said, "Nothing personal, it's just business!"

CHAPTER EIGHTEEN
THE FLIGHT TO FREEDOM

"Freedom means the supremacy of human rights everywhere.
Our support goes out to those who struggle to gain those rights
or keep them. Our strength is our unity of purpose.
To that high concept there can be no end save victory."
—Franklin D. Roosevelt

As we escaped the danger below and climbed above 5,000 feet, Pumpkin gave us the heading to fly to Chièvres Airfield in Belgium. I had Willy take control and fly the plane, then turned my attention to Bucky's status. Crisco was sitting on the floor of the rear cockpit behind us, tending to him. She had the back of Bucky's head in her lap, and was softly caressing his head and hair. She had cleaned the blood off his forehead. As I knelt down beside the two of them, I tried to examine his wound. I could see that a bullet had actually grazed his left temple and left a crease in the flesh of his scalp, but not a bullet hole. Bucky was moaning and groaning like he was talking in his sleep. I started to check his pulse to see if it was strong and regular. At that moment, he opened his eyes; looking straight into Crisco's eyes, he said, "It's so sweet of you to hold my hand like that."

The next voice he heard was mine; trying to sound feminine, I said, "It's not Crisco holding your hand; it's me, BB!" That got Bucky's immediate attention. He pulled his hand away and squirmed a bit, kicking with both legs. I commented, "It's great to see you moving your arms and legs there, Captain Jack 'Bucky' Smith!"

Jack started to speak again, "What happened? Why does the left side of my head feel like it's on fire? And why do my shoulders feel so sore?"

"Bucky, you are blessed and lucky to be alive. God's not ready for you and the devil won't have you. We might have to start calling you Lucky Bucky! Just as I came back into the cockpit after we got everyone on board, a bullet hit the left side of your forehead, and you slumped over the pilot's controls with blood coming down your forehead, face, and neck. It appears that bullet just grazed your head and momentarily knocked you unconscious; for sure, you must have some kind of a concussion. But you literally came within an inch of having a bullet in your brain and waking up in the next life! The reason your shoulders feel sore is because my adrenalin was flowing like Niagara Falls at the time; I yanked you out of that pilot's seat like a toy soldier and laid you back here on the floor. I called Crisco up here to attend to you while I took the pilot's controls, and Willy became the copilot. We then shot our way the hell out of there and took off. Pumpkin has us on a course to Chièvres Airfield in Belgium. We have thirteen folks that we rescued from the Holocaust on board the plane, all safe and soon to be set free in Belgium," I explained in a rush.

Bucky blinked for a moment, then looked at me with a tad more clarity and asked, "*You* flew us out of there?"

I replied, "Yep, and I invented a new ground maneuver for the B-17 instruction manual, called the fifty-caliber hula-hoop from hell maneuver!"

Bucky smiled and said, "I am not sure I want to know what that is, or was, but I am happy to be alive and glad we are back in the air! Who is flying the plane now?"

"I mentioned it a minute ago, but you are still groggy. Willy is our copilot, and is currently flying the plane. We are leveling at an altitude of about eleven thousand feet. With all our passengers on board, we need to keep to an altitude where we can all breathe without needing oxygen. We have a date to keep with infamy in a couple of hours at Kortenberg, Belgium, after we make a quick stop at Chièvres Airfield to free our Holocaust survivors.

"Crisco's mother is a nurse, so she is a natural to be our flight nurse for this mission. She brought our medical bag with her to attend to you. Since you are already a bit groggy from the bullet wound to your forehead, this would be a great time for me to replace your non-functioning global cosmic positioning device with a new one. Remember, I am not only your copilot, I am also your butt doctor today! So roll over and show me the scar on your buttocks, please."

Bucky was not in much of a mood to argue; he rolled on his left side, pulled down his pants, and exposed his right butt cheek. There was a jagged lightning bolt of a scar right over his GCPD incision site, exactly where he got struck coming through the white hole time tunnel. I put on sterile gloves and had Crisco draw up a syringe of lidocaine, then proceeded to numb his ass but good for the procedure. She handed me the scalpel, and I made a new incision right over the old one. Just as I was completing the incision, Pumpkin appeared on the scene.

When he saw me using the scalpel and Bucky bleeding, Pumpkin turned white as a sheet for the third time that day. He said, "Oh, *shit!*" in his proper British accent, giving the phrase extra hilarity. I told him to sit the heck down and be quiet, struggling to contain a fit of giggles.

I plucked the original GCPD out, wrapped it in some gauze, and put it in the bottom of the medical bag. Crisco opened one of the three extra GCPD boxes that we were carrying, and I put a new GCPD in the place of Bucky's old one, then quickly sutured the wound closed; the whole procedure took less than ten minutes. I told Bucky to stay down and rest for a while, and had Crisco get some water for him to drink.

I looked at Pumpkin and asked him why he had come to the cockpit. He indicated that he had been worried about Bucky, and I realized that in my haste, I hadn't given the rest of the crew an update about Bucky's condition. I grabbed the pilot's headset and got on the intercom to update the crew.

"Hey everyone, I need to let you know that Bucky is going to be OK! That German bullet shot into our cockpit came within an inch of taking his life, but it just grazed his left temple. It left him briefly unconscious, with a slight concussion. He is now awake and recovering, and I have just swapped his broken GCPD for a new one."

Tater drawled, "That poor Bucky is probably so confused right now that he doesn't know whether to check his ass or scratch his watch." The whole crew erupted in relieved laughter. When it tapered off, I asked Meatball to come to the cockpit to give me a status report about the people we had rescued.

Meatball came to the cockpit holding the hand of the eight-year-old orphan boy named Benzion 'Ben' Kaplan. Looking at both me and Pumpkin, Meatball softly introduced Ben to us. "Hey guys, this is my new friend Benzion Kaplan; Ben is from Lodz, Poland. He was an orphan at birth, and adopted by Jewish parents—who were both killed by the Nazis. He got shipped to Kolo, Poland and brought by train to Chelmno with several of the other people we just rescued. He was taken to the church in Chelmno with the twelve other prisoners on Saturday.

We all spent the night there, and we were being transported by truck to the Chelmno camp for execution on Sunday. Goondoggy, the Pud, and Crazy Ike rescued all of us as we were en route to the execution camp. We stole the truck and hid at a country summer home near your landing zone until this morning. His name, Benzion, means 'Son of Zion,' and is an expression of pining for the Jewish nation to return to its homeland: Israel, and especially Jerusalem. His last name, Kaplan, refers to the priestly workers who served in the Temple in Jerusalem." Ben appeared sad and a little bit afraid, but was looking all around the cockpit as well.

Pumpkin jumped into the conversation. Looking at Ben, he said, "You know what, Ben? I was an orphan at birth and adopted, too. My parents who adopted me were both killed one night last year, when the Nazis bombed London. You and I have a lot in common."

Ben, looking somewhat more relaxed, asked, "Why do they call you, Pumpkin?"

"Because I was the smartest kid in the patch!" Pumpkin replied.

Ben smiled and said, "No way!"

"Because I was the *strongest* kid in the patch!" Pumpkin said.

Ben, now with a big smile, said, "I think you need to try again!"

Pumpkin came clean at this point. "OK, Ben; when I get embarrassed, my round face turns orange instead of red!" And with that, Pumpkin's face started to glow a bit orange in color, and we all laughed. You could tell that there was chemistry between Pumpkin and Ben. Pumpkin then asked Ben, "What do you want to be when you grow up?"

Ben replied, "I think I want to fly planes like this one! This is the neatest thing I've ever done! I know I am good in math, so I want to do something with that, too."

What happened next was one of those moments of hope and destiny that defy gravity. Pumpkin looked at Ben and said, "I have an idea, Ben. How about you and I get together? I can adopt you, and teach you all the things I wish I would have known when I was your age and growing up—including all there is to know about airplanes and flying."

Ben, now seeming nearly at home, smiled and said, "I'd like that, Pumpkin—and I promise to try and stay in the pumpkin patch, instead of the briar patch!" We all laughed and cried simultaneously, witnesses to one of those little miracles of life and peace in a time of loss and turmoil.

Willy, who was flying the plane and eavesdropping on the conversation, turned his head and said to me, "OK, BB, that speaks for the last GCPD, just so you know. And Ben, your new dad sure knows how to find his way through the clouds and get us just where we need to go! Speaking of which, Pumpkin, I need you to recheck our heading and airspeed calculation, and make sure that we are in a straight line to Chièvres Airfield in Belgium. Our schedule is starting to get a bit tight up here; we still need to land there, drop off our passengers, take off again, and land at Kortenberg, Belgium by four PM sharp. You don't know how obsessive-compulsive Bowmar is; he is going to have his finger quivering on the white hole launch-return button, counting down the seconds to four PM. We need to have this plane on the ground in Kortenberg at four PM, or its gonna crash with us gone—and I don't want to chance changing that part of history!"

Bucky, who was still pretty groggy, chimed-in, "There's that name Bowmar again; who the hell is Bowmar, anyway?"

I looked at Bucky and said, "Well first of all, Bowmar is Cleopatra's younger brother. His IQ puts him squarely in the genius category. While Cleopatra is a social genius, her brother's brain keeps him in orbit most of the time; I'm just smart enough to understand him. He and I together figured out how to use the white hole time machine. Basically, it's like he floats around in space and I hold his ankle and connect him to the ground. It's a perfect relationship for tackling very complicated stuff, like time travel! Right now, we can use the time machine to travel back to 1942 through 1945. Bowmar and I believe that the white hole time machine could be updated using modern technology, and that it could be used to travel anytime into the past or future. But there is an even more crazy potential for the time machine." I paused and saw I had everyone's undivided attention. "Time and space are interlinked; we believe that this technology could be used for interstellar space travel to galaxies near and far. We are using exotic matter that was taken from an alien spacecraft for time travel. We are all but certain that exotic matter can be exploited for space travel, too. Pumpkin, how would you like to learn how to navigate interstellar space? And Bucky, how would you like to expand your special ops training to outer space?" Everyone in the cockpit was flabbergasted and speechless! They all knew that time travel was supposed to be impossible; yet there we were, flying in a B-17 Flying Fortress named Bad Love, on November 21, 1944. Since we had proven time travel was possible, then surely interstellar space travel was also possible.

I switched gears and asked Pumpkin if he had gotten Willy what he needed to continue directly on course to Chièvres Airfield. Pumpkin acknowledged that Willy was in good shape and we were now a little less than an hour away from Chièvres. I then surprised Pumpkin and told him and his new adopted son, Ben, that it was time to lie down for a few minutes and get their GCPDs implanted in their buttocks. Fortunately, Ben wasn't really sure what that meant; Pumpkin turned his usual shade of pale, with just a touch of orange.

I wanted to get that to-do item checked off my list in advance of landing in Chièvres. I knew that we would be in a hurry to drop off our rescued passengers, then turn around and take off again to get to Kortenberg by 4:00 PM sharp. Both Pumpkin and Ben complied, and

Crisco assisted me with the GCPD implant procedure. Bucky continued resting, and Willy flew the plane.

While I played doctor for the next 20 minutes, I had Meatball stay and give me the lowdown on all the rest of the folks that we had just rescued. As Meatball gave me the details, I went to work. Using plenty of lidocaine made the procedure as painless as possible for Ben and Pumpkin. I came to the realization that numbing the buttocks with lidocaine for implanting the GCPDs helped the procedure not cause much discomfort, the incision did not bleed too much, there was ample room for the small implantable device, and people got used to it being there; those White Hole Project people who wrote the instructions for implanting the GCPDs in the buttocks back in the '40s knew what they were doing. Crisco and I were now the world's leading experts at surgically implanting GCPDs, and we were still in high school!

When I finished, I said, "You two are all set to travel back with us to 1974 Oak Ridge, Tennessee, in just a little while!" Pumpkin and Ben hugged each other, and Pumpkin immediately started sharing his life and hopes with Ben. For his part, Ben was coming out of his shell, talking more and more. I needed to keep moving.

I checked on Willy, and he reassured me that he was truly enjoying flying a real B-17; he actually had the autopilot engaged for a while. I told him that I was headed to the back of the plane to meet our other twelve rescued passengers and explain to them our next steps. Bucky was improving with Crisco's expert nursing care, and I'm sure enjoying every moment of it as well. I told Willy if he needed anything to call for me, or to get Bucky to help in a pinch.

As I left the cockpit, I yelled at Waldo to come and join me. We headed to the back of the plane with Meatball to meet everyone and do some explaining; we needed to get everyone ready to depart the plane at Chièvres Airfield. As we passed the bomb bay compartment, we realized it was pretty cramped quarters, with twelve people sitting between the bomb bay compartment and the tail gunner location. The three of us took the time to shake everyone's hands and give big hugs. Everyone was smiling and laughing, tears of joy and tremendous thankfulness on their faces. I noticed a lot of chocolate candy wrappers on the floor, and all the parachutes were lined up along the fuselage. Amidst all this, Vadoma Loveridge kept batting her eyes at me; Hannah Lieb and Meatball were totally lovey-dovey, like newlyweds.

I asked for everyone's attention and spoke loud enough that they all could hear me. "All twelve of you—and the orphan boy, Ben Kaplan— were scheduled to be exterminated at the Chelmno camp because ten of you are Jewish, and two of you are of Gypsy heritage. You've already been told that we are time travelers from the year 1974. All of us who came here to rescue you know the truth. You were part of what will one day be called the Holocaust; at Chelmno alone, roughly three hundred forty thousand souls lost their lives, dying by poison carbon monoxide gas, and were then cremated. It is estimated that more than six million people were killed in the Holocaust, in an attempt at genocide of the Jews and Gypsies, during this World War that is going to end in 1945. When we discovered time travel, we made it our first mission, to save some Holocaust souls from certain death; we managed to save the thirteen of you on this very day. We all agreed that even if we only saved a single life from the Holocaust, this day would be worth it—because who can put a value on a single precious life saved? All of you have made all of us feel and experience a sense of truth about what really happened during this time in history. We will never forget all of you and your stories, and our lives are changed forever!"

I continued, "Because our mission is secret and no one but us knows that time travel is possible, I have to swear all of you to secrecy— not that anyone would necessarily believe you, but we are not sure what happens when history gets changed. We think this mission will create a small wrinkle in time, but this is our very first mission, and we are not done. So I am pleading with you not to share this rescue story with outsiders. We will try to keep an eye on your whereabouts, but do not want to try and change your destiny again. However, it is God that brought us together at this time and place by fate, and if we ever cross paths again by fate, you can use the code words *Bad Love* as a test. We will know that we have met, and that we are connected by fate."

The spry and spunky Avigail Goldberg spoke up. "BB, I am the old gal in this crowd, and I want you to know that we dearly love and are beyond thankful for you and the entire Bad Love gang. But I want to know, why are you called the Bad Love Gang?" I answered, "Well, Avigail, that is an interesting question, and I guess that I am not totally surprised that you asked!" Just as I was starting to speak, I could hear the background music of Isaac Hayes' 1971 hit **"Theme from Shaft"** playing in my music brain.

I then continued, "So where—when—we come from in 1974, the definition, interpretation, or meaning of some basic words has changed a bit from what you're used to here in the Forties. For example, the phrase *Can you dig it?* means *Do you understand?* There's a Jewish slang word where you call someone who is constantly screwing up a putz. We've even taken the word *bitch* and turned it into *bitchin'*, which means *the all time best, way cool,* and *really neat.* Like we would say, 'This plane is bitchin'!' In 1974, the word *bad* means *very, very good, awesome,* or *totally cool.* Our gang of friends grew up together, since the 1960s; despite all of our differences, we all love each other and would go to the mat for each other—so we called ourselves the Bad Love Gang. Does that make any sense to you now, Avigail?"

Avigail looked at her husband Asher, then looked at me and replied, "Yes, BB, I can dig it. And even though Asher is a putz once in a while, he better not call me bitchin', or he's gonna find out what a bad mother his wife is!" We all busted a gut laughing at Avigail's amazing wit, and I exclaimed, "Well, I guess that explains *that!*"

Willy then called down from the cockpit over the intercom to Cleopatra to tell her we were approaching Chièvres Airfield, and that I needed to get back to the pilot's seat. She told me that Willy was calling for me, but before I went back up to the cockpit, I told Waldo to get his Major General Paul Thompson persona ready for action. He would stay with our twelve rescued passengers, get off the plane with them, and be prepared to explain to whoever met us that we were on a secret mission and delivering these folks to safety and freedom. Waldo looked me in the eye and said, "No problem, BB. Get your ass back in the pilot seat and land this thing!" For another brief moment, I thought I was in a John Wayne war movie.

I made my way back up to the cockpit and immediately checked on Bucky. He was awake and resting, with Crisco still at his side. I asked him if he was ready to help. He told me he could help, but still felt a bit off balance and would rather be copilot for now. I reassured him that this was the plan anyway as Crisco and I helped him to his feet. Willy reengaged the autopilot for a minute while I got into the pilot's seat, then Willy and Crisco assisted Bucky into the copilot's seat. We both got our headgear on and I asked Bucky and Pumpkin to radio the Chièvres Airfield Tower with our identifying colors and letters for that day, and get us cleared to land. The Chièvres runway was plenty long, and much easier than landing on a farmer's field in Chelmno, Poland marked by leafy tree branches! We lowered our landing gear and flaps as we came in at 150 MPH, slowing to 105 MPH as we passed over the airfield boundary. We touched down at 95 MPH and made a smooth 3-point landing—only this time, we landed at an American-held airbase that had been recaptured from the Germans in early September 1944.

As we taxied to the other end of the runway, we could see P-47D Thunderbolts, P-51 Mustangs, and Hawker Typhoons all parked off to the side, standing ready to fly and fight. It gave me goosebumps, seeing all this Allied airpower in real life, ready to go in what I knew to be the waning months of the WWII European Theater. I told Frankie to unlock the tail wheel, then we made a turn at the end of the runway. I pointed Bad Love right back out in the direction we had landed, and left the four Wright Cyclone engines idling; I loved this plane! I could see a regular U.S. Army jeep and a maintenance truck headed in our direction. For maybe the first time since we left Oak Ridge earlier that day, I felt safe and relieved.

I got on the intercom and said, "Everyone listen up, this is important. Waldo is going to greet the local military ground crew and explain that we are on a secret mission, just here on the ground for a few minutes to drop off our twelve Jewish and Gypsy Holocaust victims to safety and freedom. Goondoggy and Crazy Ike, you two get out and assist our passengers off the plane. And make sure that Meatball gets back on this plane after he says goodbye to Hannah; that boy has stars in his eyes! Willy, you and the Pud take the stepladder and peel the Bad Love emblem off of the plane. Remember, this plane has no official name when we land in Kortenberg! Pumpkin, you and Ben stay put and get our navigation coordinates planned to get us to Kortenberg as soon as we leave here. Bucky, you keep the plane idling while I go out and make sure I haven't forgotten anything."

Daniel, Mazal, Zelda, and Rhoda Roth, along with Mazal's mother, Rachel Soros, were the first to exit the plane. Daniel immediately got down on his knees and kissed the free Belgium ground. David and Sarah Lieb were next, followed by their daughter Hannah—with Meatball in tow, holding her hand. Then the elderly couple, Asher and Avigail Goldberg, made it off. Vadoma and Barsali Loveridge were the last of the twelve rescued passengers to exit. As I got off the plane from the front, I could see that Waldo had already spoken to the ground crew and was walking back toward me. Waldo came directly up to me and said, "BB, all these army guys are so young! I must look ancient like Moses or something, because I didn't even have to show them my fake orders; they just saluted and believed everything that I had to say!" I asked if they were ready and able to help our twelve rescued souls. Waldo answered, "They are actually excited and relieved to help our rescued folks. Apparently, they have mainly been getting German prisoners of war to process through here, and have set up a German POW camp. I told them to process our twelve rescued Holocaust victims with the greatest of care, giving them everything they need—and that was 'an order.' They replied, 'Yes sir, General! Is there anything else, General?' I was thinking to myself that maybe I could get used to this command and control way of life!"

To that I replied, "Not so long as we are in your life; you're just Waldo to us! Get on the plane, General!"

I turned and walked to the group of twelve, who were all hugging and shaking hands. I gave all of them great big hugs, wished them all well, and reassured them that Waldo had paved the way for them to immediately get the help that they needed to keep moving forward with their lives and futures. They all turned and headed to the parked jeep and army truck. The Pud and Willy had taken the Bad Love emblem off of the fuselage and were getting back on board the plane. I looked at Crazy Ike and Goondoggy, who were leaning against the back of the plane staring at something; they pointed to the objects of their attention. It was Meatball and Hannah, embraced tightly in what might have been construed as a permanent lip lock! I yelled for Sarah Lieb (Hannah's mother) and ran over to her. I asked Sarah to come with me, in case we had to literally pry Meatball and Hannah apart. It was time for us to leave.

Sarah and I walked over to Hannah and Meatball; God, it was sad. They were both in tears.

Meatball looked at me and said, "BB, I can't leave her!"

"Mom, I love him so much!" Hannah sobbed to her mother.

Sarah softly said, "Sweetheart, I am so sorry, but you need to stay here with your father and me."

I was thinking, *they just met three days ago, and I have to take Meatball back to 1974!* I tried to be objective and said, "Meatball, we have no more GCPDs; we couldn't take Hannah with us even if we wanted to. You just met Hannah three days ago, and she needs to stay here with her family. We need to get on the plane now."

Meatball looked at me with fire and fury in his eyes and said, "I hate you, BB!"

I replied, "I hate you too, Meatball; now come and get on the plane with me!" I started to motion for Crazy Ike and Goondoggy, but Meatball capitulated.

"OK, at least let us kiss goodbye," he said sadly. Sarah and I stepped aside and turned our backs to them for a little privacy. I told Sarah that she had a beautiful daughter, and that I hated to separate her and Meatball. Sarah thanked and hugged me again, and I could appreciate and sense that Hannah was from a strong family; she would be just fine after we left. Meatball then tapped me on the shoulder and said, "Let's go, before I get sick and die!" We turned and ran to the plane, but something I could not explain tugged at my soul. I shook it off, knowing we needed to keep moving.

CHAPTER NINETEEN
THE FLIGHT TO DESTINY

"Life is like riding a bicycle. To keep your balance
you must keep moving."
—Albert Einstein

W e were all back aboard the aircraft once again known as #545, the
plane with no name (the Bad Love decal had been taken down),
on its third mission ever. I sat in the pilot's seat and asked Bucky how
he was feeling; he had a whopper of a headache, but was otherwise
good to go. Putting my headgear on, I had everyone check in. We now
had fifteen people on board, and all of us had global cosmic positioning devices implanted in our butt cheeks. Bucky radioed the tower
and learned they had already been alerted by the ground crew that we
were carrying a two-star major general; they knew we were on the last
leg of a secret mission, having dropped off twelve rescued passengers,
and were turning to take off. The tower gave us permission to taxi to
our takeoff position, and then instructed us to hold for another plane
to land. We taxied as directed and once in position, I plugged a new
cassette into Marantz Superscope C200 and showed Bucky how to hit
the *play* button, when I told him to do so.

"All right, Bad Love Crew, we are headed to Kortenberg for a rendezvous with the destiny of time travel. It seems like a long time ago that we arrived in England to commandeer this plane, but that was only five thirty this morning. We lost an hour flying east today; now we are on a very tight schedule to get to Kortenberg and land exactly at four PM. Fortunately, we are only about sixty miles away from our landing spot, and Pumpkin's got us all dialed-in to fly there pronto," I announced.

Tater came on the intercom and blurted out, "We'll get there faster than a one-legged man loses a butt-kicking contest."

We all laughed and I replied, "Assuming Tater is correct, and we land in Kortenberg with a minute or two to spare, let's all gather between the bomb bay and the rear of the plane so we are grouped together for the time travel back. No one is coming to investigate the plane for about twenty minutes after we land, so potentially we have a little window of time—no pun intended—to gather. The landing in Kortenberg will be rough; it is a plowed field, not a nicely groomed runway. If we do this right, one of wings will dip as we are at the end of our landing. This will destroy one of the propellers and flip us around to a standstill, but the other three engines will keep running."

Pumpkin asked what should have been an obvious question for everyone else. "Since I am new to this white hole time travel thing, what happens if we are not all grouped together to make the return trip? What happens if we are not on the ground when the clock strikes four PM?"

I answered, "Great question, Pumpkin, and one that Bowmar and I have spent a lot of time pondering. We believe that the GPCDs can track you, and all of us who have GCPDs, no matter where you are located. Once you are recalled, you are going back specifically to the Oak Ridge White Hole Project time machine in 1974, no matter what.

That is where your matching GCPD is locked into the time travel control panel. At four PM, all of us go back—regardless of our relative location. I am just being a little cautious about us grouping together, if we get the chance to do so."

I continued, "Let me give you an extreme example: Bowmar and I believe that if you fell out of this plane at three fifty-nine PM, so long as you didn't hit the ground before four PM, you would be zapped back in time to Oak Ridge, Tennessee mid-flight, along with the rest of us who were still on the plane. Your downward velocity at the time you were zapped into the time tunnel should normalize with the rest of us. The time travel re-entry platform is soft and forgiving, so hopefully you would land safely with the rest of us."

Crisco said, "BB, my emotions about getting home safe are never soothed by you saying something like, 'hopefully we'll land safely!'"

I replied, "Point your butt downward and you'll land safe, Crisco!"

She looked at Cleopatra and said, "We're going to kill him when we get back!"

"Insofar as the plane is concerned, if we are still in the air at four PM, we all get zapped back to 1974, and the plane is on its own after that," I concluded.

Bucky was listening to the tower chatter, and we were soon cleared for takeoff. I made the final 90 degree turn onto the runway, then told Frankie to lock the tail wheel for the last time. I said, "Here we go, and I have one of my favorite Three Dog Night songs, appropriate for time travel, coming on for a little takeoff entertainment!" I stood on the brakes and Bucky and I throttled up the four Wright Cyclones for takeoff. We powered down the runway as soon as I released the brakes. I told Bucky to hit the *play* button, and all our headphones were filled with Three Dog Night's **"Shambala,"** which had peaked at #3 on the U.S Billboard Hot 100 Chart in 1973. We reached 125 MPH and I pulled the wheel back. taking us back into the sky over allied Belgium on a quick course to Kortenberg as the crew lip synced that we were on the road to "Shambala."

As the song ended, I had Bucky hit the *stop* button on the Marantz cassette player, and told everyone to pack up all that we brought except for the current, 1944 candy wrappers that were laying around everywhere, and all the parachutes that were neatly stacked along the inside fuselage. I instructed Pumpkin to leave the bomber's log and daily code book open on the navigator's desk. I reminded Waldo to leave the Sperry bombsight cover sitting neatly beside it. I told everyone to leave everything as we had found it, including any flight jackets. This was going to be a very short flight!

Pumpkin had been working on exact coordinates for our landing in the Kortenberg Royal Air Force airfield. He came to the cockpit, and we were all getting very nervous because it was 3:53 PM; we were ten miles out, and coming in hot. We were perfectly aligned with Pumpkin's navigation coordinates. Suddenly, we could see the antiaircraft unit and the plowed field directly ahead. I told the crew to brace for a rough landing, and for time travel!

For the second time that day, adrenalin poured into my veins and rushed through my system; time seemed to slow down, like we were in a movie scene done in slow motion. We had already lowered the landing gear and flaps, so we brought the approach airspeed down to 105 MPH. We flew right by the antiaircraft position, and I swear the British soldiers could see us through the cockpit window. It was so surreal that it felt like an out-of-body experience.

We touched down hard in the plowed field, going 90 MPH at the moment our wheels touched the ground. I struggled to keep the plane straight as we bounced a few times, and simultaneously applied the brakes hard. Just as I thought we were slowing down nicely and getting better control, we must have rolled through a ditch or hit a hole. One of the wings hit the ground, catching the propeller and swinging the whole plane around. At that instant, my world went white...as did the world for the fourteen other time travelers on board The Phantom Fortress.

CHAPTER TWENTY
MISSION COMPLETED

"Put your hand on a hot stove for a minute, and it seems like an hour. Sit with a pretty girl for an hour, and it seems like a minute. That's relativity."
—Albert Einstein

O n the morning of November 21, 1974, at the White Hole Project time machine, Bowmar had aligned and locked the upper race-track of the time tunnel to November 21, 1944 and then engaged the light speed drive. He next docked the telescopic, exotic matter-lined funnel connecting the lower racetrack with the upper racetrack, and powered on the lower racetrack and all the control panels. All fifteen GCPDs allowed by the White Hole Project time machine were pre-cisely docked and locked in place in the mission control panel. Each of those individual GCPDs was part of a matching pair, with the match-ing GCPD implanted in each one of us. With the exception of the extra three GCPDs that we took on the mission, Bowmar had labeled each of the GCPD docking sites with the name of the person that GCPD and docking site represented.

At precisely 10:00 AM on November 21, 1974 in Oak Ridge, Ten-nessee (that was 4:00 PM in Kortenberg, Belgium), Bowmar hit the time traveler recall button on the mission control panel. From Bowmar's perspective, the machine made an unusually deep humming noise and whirring sound combined, seeming harmoniously linked. The deep humming noise seemed to be emanating from the exotic matter-lined funnel connecting the two racetracks. From Bowmar's point of view, the results after hitting the recall button seemed nearly instantaneous.

From my perspective, and that of the other fourteen time travelers, the time travel process in no way matched what Hollywood or television shows had made it out to be. It was a totally different experience! Just as the clock struck 4:00 PM in Kortenberg, we were on the ground near the end of our landing roll; the wing of our B-17 had dipped and dug into the earth, causing one of the propellers to buckle and the plane to ground loop, coming to a complete stop. As all of us aboard the B-17 were swinging around in that ground loop semicircle, Bowmar hit the time traveler recall button on the mission control panel and our world instantly turned white. As the fifteen of us vanished, the air inside the plane was like a primordial mixture smelling of fire, water, and exotic matter. This time, given the fact that fifteen time travelers were zapped away, the odor lingered for a while.

The experience of traveling back to the future to 1974 Oak Ridge, Tennessee, was pure white, serene, and heavenly peaceful—with one exception. There were intermittent bolts of lightning in the tunnel that were brighter than the white, but there was no thunder or scary noise as you might expect. It was quiet lightning that seemed to be a natural part of process, not something we perceived as threatening or dangerous...unless or until it touched you. If that happened, it stung and left you with a unique lightning bolt scar, like a mark of glory from the universe of time travel.

On the trip to 1944 England earlier that day, I had kept my eyes open. On the trip back to 1974 Oak Ridge, I closed my eyes and saw a vision. I was a little boy again, about age seven. I woke up in my bed in our home in Oak Ridge, Tennessee as a child. When I opened my eyes, I saw that it was a beautiful, sunny day with blue skies and puffy white clouds. The temperature was perfect, and I found myself walking in the street in front of our house. There was a soft breeze whispering through the silvery green leaves of the tree next to me. I said "Hi" to our next-door neighbor, who was working in her yard. It was so incredibly innocent, peaceful and tranquil...

And then I hit the soft, comfy-cozy, padded circular eye of the ground floor time machine racetrack, and opened my eyes involuntarily. The other fourteen time travelers were all sitting or lying there with me. We were back! We hugged and cried our eyes out in that moment of incredible joy and victory. Bowmar undocked and raised the telescopic, exotic matter-lined funnel to open the machine, then jumped in with us. It was an indescribable moment of happiness, relief, and accomplishment for all of us.

The twelve of us time travelers from our Bad Love Gang who went on this Holocaust rescue mission had thought that we were the first known humans to travel in time. Actually, Captain Jack "Bucky" Smith was the first known human to travel in time from the White Hole Project time machine; he was launched on March 14, 1945, from Oak Ridge, Tennessee to the East Anglia Airbase in England by our predecessors. His GCPD got freakishly struck by the whiter-than-white lightning and was irreparably damaged on that inaugural time travel launch.

Bucky had been stuck in time, although we were betting they had desperately tried to bring him back. However, with his GCPD knocked out, the first test was a failure; they couldn't get him back, and must have assumed that Bucky was killed, or lost somewhere in time. With FDR's unexpected death, the historic Manhattan Project and the world's first atomic bomb nearly built and to be successfully tested by the United States a few months later in 1945, someone had secretly cancelled the White Hole Project. The Manhattan Project was so top secret that Vice President Harry Truman didn't know about it until he was sworn into office as president and briefed after President Franklin D. Roosevelt's death. The White Hole Project was so super-top-secret that the knowledge of its existence somehow went to the grave with FDR and anyone else who knew about it.

Or so we surmised...

At any rate, the twelve of us time travelers from the Bad Love Gang, along with Bucky, could at least say that we were the first known humans to travel back in time and safely return. Bucky's return was certainly delayed, but he did not perceive that delay or age in the process. Pumpkin and Ben could say they were among the first to safely time travel in one direction. What we couldn't tell the world—or anyone, outside of our inner circle—was that not only did we go back in time and return, we also conducted a rescue mission that meant the world to us, and to the thirteen people whom we rescued.

EPILOGUE

"OK, I will admit that I am having some memory issues.
I can do pretty good with the past,
It's the future I have trouble remembering..."
—Larry W. Schewe

One Year Later: November 1975

Bowmar and I had summoned Meatball to come to my parent's home for some important information, and to help us decide whether or not to act on what we had discovered. He was in the middle of lifting weights in his basement when we called. Based on the serious tone of my voice, he came over right away.

"So, Butt Head... I mean, Bubble Butt, and Bowmar...what is so critical that you two had to interrupt my all-important body beautification workout, to get me here in person?"

I led the discussion, although it was Bowmar's research that had led to this revelation. "You know how we all agreed to do our best to keep track of anyone we rescued, to build a database in case our time travels created anything more than a slight wrinkle in time? Well, Bowmar and his stellar I.Q."...Bowmar looked surprised that I had given him an actual compliment..."have managed to do a great job of tracking our rescued Holocaust folks, but we just got this new information."

Meatball acknowledged the question with a wave. "Yes, of course I remember; but what does this have to do with me?"

I continued, "The Jewish girl Hannah Lieb, who you fell head over heels in love with, and who we had to literally pry you away from to get you back on the plane... We have found her, and the news is not good. Only one year has passed for all of us, but thirty-one years have passed for Hannah and her family. We have just discovered that she and her family are living in Jerusalem, Israel. She is now forty-nine years old, and she is dying of breast cancer that has spread throughout her body. She is on a lot of pain medications, and her level of consciousness is fading in and out. She is calling out 'Bad Love, come back!' and 'Meatball!' She is not married, as best we know, and her family is at a loss on how to help her in these final days of her life. They are also concerned that other people who might hear her will start asking questions, and that in her altered level of consciousness, she might divulge her secrets. Bowmar and I have discussed this thoroughly, and we think that you need to head over to Jerusalem ASAP. Waldo has been briefed, and he is concerned enough that he will pay for your trip."

Jerusalem, Israel: Five Days Later

The Liebs lived in the heart of Jerusalem on well-known King David Street. Hannah's father, David Lieb, had moved the family to Jerusalem in late 1946 and started a road and building construction company with two of his cousins. They were very successful, and still going strong in 1975. Hannah had her own two-bedroom apartment down the street from the famous King David Hotel, where Waldo had made Meatball a reservation for the lowest-priced room available (which was still no bargain). Meatball checked in, took a shower, and headed to Hannah's apartment on foot. I had paved the way for the Liebs to be prepared for and expecting Meatball by calling ahead of time and connecting with Hannah's mother, Sarah Lieb. They were truly excited to hear from us, and to be able to see Meatball again, but that excitement was muted by the circumstances of Hannah's losing battle against metastatic breast cancer.

Meatball arrived at Hannah's apartment just before sunset. David and Sarah met him at the front door with tears and hugs, astonished that they were 31 years older, but Meatball was only one year older: age seventeen. They took him to Hannah's bedroom and there she was: sitting up on her bed, wearing blue jeans and a white button-down blouse. She had refused chemotherapy, which was more toxic than medicinal in 1975. He smiled when he saw that she still had her beautiful head of wavy, dark brown hair. Although she was now 49 years old and appeared somewhat thin, she was still beyond beautiful in Meatball's eyes.

Hannah immediately recognized him and loudly exclaimed, "*Meatball*"! Her eyes filled with light and sparkle, for the first time in six months. They embraced and were in the middle of a long kiss when Hannah's nurse, Ruth—an older, heavyset, but jovial lady—came around the corner and witnessed the lip lock. David and Sarah quickly lied to Ruth, telling her that Meatball was Hannah's nephew, Aaron. Ruth quipped, "I guess they are pretty close, huh?"

Hannah held Aaron at arm's length and explained, "Meatball, I don't have long to live, and the pain medicine is affecting my sense of time and ability to concentrate. I have struggled to hold on and hoped that you could make it here in time, so that I could be the one to tell you..." Her eyes were full of tears, but she was also smiling.

Meatball was also crying, and asked, "What do you have to tell me, Hannah?"

Hannah said, "Well, you remember our afternoon of passionate love by the pond in Poland, Aaron?"

"Like it was yesterday and forever, Hannah!"

Hannah paused for a minute and then said, "Well, it is a bit like forever, Aaron, because I have someone you need to meet. Elijah, come in here!" Meatball looked at the doorway, and in walked a 30-year-old Incredible Hulk of a chiseled man with a kind, welcoming face, wearing Israeli military clothing and insignia indicating he was in the Israeli Special Defense Forces. Hannah says, "Elijah, meet your seventeen-year-old father, Meatball!"

That same moment, at BB's home in Oak Ridge, Tennessee...

Bubble Butt's parents were gone and he was lying on his bed just about to doze off for a nap, but he suddenly heard new music playing: **"Never Been Any Reason"** by Head East, from the *Flat as a Pancake* album. BB immediately liked what he heard, and also knew that it was brand new for 1975. He also realized he did not yet own that album, and that he had not turned the stereo on when he lay down to rest. Somewhat confused, he rolled over, and standing at his bedside three feet away was a man with a familiar face: his own, but at age 62.

"Well, well, Bubble Brat, I mean Bubble Butt, here you are...and here I am, at age sixty-two. You're gonna really like this entire *Flat as a Pancake* album by Head East! You should know that the great German physicists said this would be either impossible or absurd, to travel back in time and have a discussion with your younger self. I will not tell you what happens in the future, but I am going to give you a few principles to hopefully guide you better as you tackle the future. We've got ten minutes, so listen carefully..."

COMING SOON

THE BAD LOVE SERIES

The Bad Love Gang are the first known humans to travel back in time and safely return, but this is only their inaugural mission. They now suspect that time travel and interstellar space travel are intimately interconnected and that the discovery of exotic matter somehow holds the key to unlock this mystery. One thing is for certain: their lives are forever changed, and rescue will be the motivation and theme for all their future missions.

ABOUT THE AUTHOR

Kevin L. Schewe, MD, FACRO, is the proud father of two daughters (Ashley and Christie) and two granddaughters (Gracie and Olivia). He is a native of St. Louis, Missouri, and now makes his home in the mile-high city of Denver, Colorado. He is a board-certified cancer specialist who has been in the private practice of radiation oncology for 32+ years. He continues to practice medicine as the Medical Director of Radiation Oncology for Alliance Cancer Care Colorado at Red Rocks in Golden, Colorado (www.accredrocks.com). He is an entrepreneur, having founded a cosmetics company called Elite Therapeutics (elitetherapeutics.com) and Bad Love Cosmetics Company, LLC. He also serves as Chairman of the Board of a small, publicly-traded, renewable, green energy and animal feed company called VIASPACE, Inc. (www.viaspace.com), which recently acquired Elite Therapeutics and Bad Love Cosmetics, LLC.

The first Sunday of June every year is National Cancer Survivor's Day. Dr. Schewe co-chairs a yearly celebration of National Cancer Survivor's Day at the Red Rocks Medical Center in Golden, Colorado. Every year, he writes a skit that he and the local doctors perform in front of the Survivor's Day crowd. The skit always has a musical theme from the 1950s, 1960s, 1970s, 1980s, or one of various Hollywood themes. The doctors, dressed in costumes for their parts, ask questions or pose dilemmas to each other. The answers to those questions or dilemmas are clips from songs, which the doctors lip sync and dance to in front of the crowd. Everyone dances together at the end of the skit. It is great fun and an uplifting celebration of survival for the cancer patients, their families, and their loved ones.

We then moved away from the entrance, walked around the perimeter of the third floor, and came to a set of double doors with signage above that read:

MEDICAL BAY
"A ship is always safe at shore,
but that is not what it is built for."
—Albert Einstein

The inside of the medical bay had two operating tables with large overhead lights. The walls were lined with white metal cabinets, glass doors revealing that the cabinets were fully stocked with medical supplies such as gloves, syringes, scalpels, suture material, etc. We noticed that one of the cabinets was marked *Implantable GCPDs*; the shelves inside were filled with these GCPDs, which were curiously packaged in numbered boxes of matching pairs. The GCPDs were spherical, shiny metal objects about the diameter of a small cherry tomato or American quarter. The boxes containing the GCPDs were labelled *First device to be implanted in the cheek of the buttocks using sterile technique, and matching device inserted in control panel prior to launch or recall.* Bowmar and I would soon discover that GCPD stood for global cosmic positioning device.

Down the hall from the Medical Bay was another set of double doors.

WARDROBE WAREHOUSE
"Courage is being scared to death...
and saddling up anyway."
—John Wayne

"Whenever I am faced with two evils,
I take the one I haven't tried before."
—Mae West

We went through the doors and to our amazement, it was a huge room with sections and rows upon rows of clothing that seemed endless. The male and female clothing was essentially arranged by nation and region, and also by World War II Army, Navy, Marine and Air Force—military forces including the United States, Britain, Australia, China, Germany, Italy, Japan, etc. In addition, there were shoes, belts, boots, medals, insignia, and rank appliques for each branch. Even more amazing, there was a small arms/firearms section correlating with each of the WWII military forces. There was civilian clothing too, for what seemed like every country or region on earth, and no detail was left out; there were coats, gloves, hats, and other accessories galore! The wardrobe warehouse alone was worth a fortune, and would leave anyone from Hollywood drooling and green with envy.

Bowmar and I then made our way down to the ground floor level marked NOW. There was an impressive control panel area in front of the lower racetrack machine, with command and control functions that seemed clearly marked. There were *power* levers for the upper and lower racetrack machines; switches marked *lower dock* and *upper dock*, presumably for the telescopic, central connector funnel; and large command buttons marked SEND and RECALL. One section of the control panel was dedicated to programing a specific global geographic location using precise coordinates of latitude, longitude, and elevation. There was also a separate section for docking and locking up to fifteen of the global cosmic positioning devices (GCPDs) in place. Bowmar and I collectively surmised that the machine could send up to a maximum of fifteen souls to the years 1942, 1943, 1944, or 1945, and then recall them back to the present time.

We then walked through a doorway going in and through the lower racetrack machine and into the central stage of the lower racetrack. This was the area that had appeared to be a comfy-cozy sunken living room covered in soft cushions that we had seen from the third floor above. Not only was it truly comfy-cozy with all the soft cushions, it also had a trampoline-like floor. The designers must have thought that the time travelers returning back through the time funnel/time tunnel might be falling back onto this stage when coming back in time. Bowmar and I jumped up and down and dove all around the central stage like a couple of little kids jumping on a soft feather bed.

"I know where I'm gonna take a nap when we spend any long hours in this place. Speaking of time travel, what do you call a sleeping dinosaur, Bowman?"

Bowmar responded, "Beats me, BB. What's the answer?"

I replied, "A dinos*nore!*"

Bowmar smiled, shook his head and said, "That's got to be one of your all-time worst jokes, BB. I'm gonna use this thing to send you back to the stone ages for that one!"

We then left the lower racetrack and walked past the control panel and into the circular ground floor hallway. As we walked around the other side, opposite the control panel area, we came to another doorway. This one was a huge steel door with a circular, submarine airlock-type latch. Above this doorway entrance there was another sign.

EXOTIC MATTER CONTAINMENT
AUTHORIZED PERSONNEL ONLY
"A new type of thinking is essential if mankind is to
survive and move toward higher levels."
—Albert Einstein

Obviously, it had been a long time since it was opened; it again took the two of us to get the heavy steel door open. Bowmar looked at me, smiled and asked, "Do you think that we are authorized to enter?"

I responded, "In the words of Henry David Thoreau 'Any fool can make a rule and any fool will mind it.' So follow me, Bowmar." We entered the room and turned on the lights. It appeared to be a large research lab of sorts, with various instruments, spectrometers, Geiger counters, weights & measures, microscopes, you name it.

As we moved through the lab towards the back of the room, we saw a rear corner office with windows situated to view out into the lab. Adjacent to the office and stacked against the back wall, there were heavy-duty crates that were all labeled *Top Secret*. These were even more interesting because each cube was about one square foot in size, and they were all stacked, numbered, and dated very neatly. We went into the office and began systematically searching the desk and the bookshelves behind the desk. Everything was in its place as if nothing had ever happened, and the next work day was ready to get started. It took some searching, but I found what appeared to be a log book.

Bowmar and I read through it together. The log book detailed the origin of the exotic matter, which had been obtained from an alien spaceship that had crashed at Indian Springs Airfield, AKA Groom Dry Lake, in the southwest Nevada desert in June of 1942. The log book also contained details on each serial numbered crate of exotic matter, and when each of those crates had been delivered to the lab. The last crate to be delivered was checked in on Tuesday, April 10, 1945. Bowmar, looked at me and said, "President Franklin D. Roosevelt died of a massive stroke in the afternoon of Thursday, April twelfth of 1945."

I stared at Bowmar and asked, "How on earth do you remember something like that?!"